The Faithfu

»»»»»»»»»»»» ««««««««««««

Stefan Żeromski

The Faithful River

TRANSLATED FROM THE POLISH

BY BILL JOHNSTON

NORTHWESTERN UNIVERSITY PRESS
EVANSTON, ILLINOIS

»»»»»»»»»»»» ««««««««««««

Northwestern University Press
Evanston, Illinois 60208-4170

First published in Polish under the title *Wierna rzeka*. English translation

Printed in the United States of America

10 9 8 7 6 5 4 3

ISBN 0-8101-1596-4

Library of Congress Cataloging-in-Publication Data

Żeromski, Stefan, 1864–1925.
[Wierna rzeka. English]
The faithful river / Stefan Zeromski ; translated from the Polish by Bill Johnston.
p. cm.
ISBN 0-8101-1596-4 (pbk.)
1. Poland—History—Revolution, 1863–1864—Fiction. I. Johnston, Bill. II. Title.
PG7158.Z4W5514 1999
891.8'536—dc21 99-27010
CIP

∞ The paper used in this publication meets the minimum requirements of the American National Standard for Information Sciences—Permanence of Paper for Printed Library Materials, ANSI Z39.48-1992.

Tłumaczenie to
pamięci Jacka Rydla
poświęcam

This translation is dedicated
to the memory of
Jacek Rydel

»»»» CONTENTS ««««

»»»» TRANSLATOR'S INTRODUCTION ««««

Stefan Żeromski (1864–1925) was the leading Polish novelist of his generation. His major novels—including *The Faithful River* (1912), *Popioły* (*Ashes*, 1904), and *Przedwiośnie* (*Before the Spring*, 1925)—are works of great ideological and formal complexity that constitute significant contributions to world literature. In his lifetime Żeromski was acknowledged as a major European writer. He was much admired, for example, by Joseph Conrad; he was mentioned as a potential Nobel laureate in 1924, and his books were widely translated into many languages.

Since then, though in Poland he continues to be regarded as one of the greatest of all Polish novelists (Czesław Miłosz calls him "the conscience of Polish literature"), he has been unfairly ignored in translation, especially into English. The present novel, one of his greatest achievements and at the same time one of his most accessible works, is aimed at redressing the balance somewhat and reintroducing Żeromski to an English-speaking audience.

The Faithful River is set in the Kielce region of central Poland in the winter and spring of 1863, during the January Uprising. At this time the country of Poland did not exist; since the partitions of the late eighteenth century its territory had been carved up by Russia, Prussia, and Austria. In January 1863 a second armed insurrection (after the November Uprising of 1830–31) broke out in the Russian-occupied part of the country, with much of the fighting concentrated in the region where the novel is set. The Poles scored some notable victories but were ultimately crushed by the might of the Russian forces. The uprising finally collapsed in the fall of 1864. It was to be the last organized revolt against any of the occupying powers until World War I, which broke out two years after the publication of this novel.

Żeromski has been dubbed the "posthumous child of the January Uprising." Born in its closing phases, he found it a compelling symbol of both the hope and the hopelessness of the Polish nationalist cause. In *The Faithful River*, a book written at a historical and geographical distance from the uprising, he confronts its paradoxes head on. He could clearly see that it had been doomed to failure from the start; yet for him, as for many Poles, there was a profound sense in which the hope lay in the struggle as much as in victory.

Complex and ambivalent attitudes to the uprising infuse every page of the book. The devotion of those who fought, from the leaders (Olbromski) to the men in the ranks (Odrowąż), is counterbalanced by the willingness of the farmspeople to turn rebels over to the authorities. The Polish insurgents who visit the manor behave in a way that can scarcely be called heroic, reduced to desperation and brutality by the exigencies of an impossible cause. The Russian officer who preys on Salomea also reads dissident literature condemning the Russian role in the rebellion. Above all, Salomea herself, the central character, is one moment fiercely patriotic, the next railing against the irresponsibility of those who instigated the uprising and the suffering it has brought in its wake.

The Faithful River, then, is a war story. Indeed, despite the fact that it was written almost fifty years after the events it describes, it has been called the greatest of all novels of the uprising (the parallels with Stephen Crane's treatment of the Civil War in his 1895

The Red Badge of Courage are intriguing). Yet Żeromski's novel is a war story unlike others. Though, somewhat incidentally, we meet soldiers, rebels, and leaders, we do not read about battles, strategy and tactics, night bivouacs, and forced marches. The action takes place not on a battlefield or in a general's tent, but in a deserted manor house where most of the time the principal matter for concern is a drastic shortage of food.

This, however, is Żeromski's true achievement. Instead of giving us the military perspective of the soldier, we see the civilian's experience of the war: the day-to-day suffering, the deprivations, the lack of food and firewood; the devastation of property; and above all the destruction the uprising wreaks upon the lives of ordinary people. Families are broken up, sons are killed, fathers go missing; wives and daughters are left behind or roam the countryside, looking for their loved ones.

In this regard, Żeromski's novel is a story for the postmodern age. Its central characters are those who in other novels of wartime do not belong on the field of battle and so are typically relegated to marginal, passive roles: a young woman and an old man. In the world of Żeromski's book the expected order is turned upside down. Odrowąż, the young soldier, is sick and unable to act; it is Salomea and the aged Szczepan who are the prime movers, and who take on the role of protagonists in the story. And, like true postmoderns, they resist the established order as much as they can—and with considerable success for the most part.

In the central figure of Salomea, Żeromski has created a truly postmodern hero. Salomea is positioned marginally by the war and also by her own society; both these forces expect her to react passively to events and to know her place. Yet she rejects such strictures, and instead actively pursues her ends under horribly difficult circumstances. Despite her physical limitations and the paucity of her resources, she is able to take in the wounded soldier, nurse him, feed him, and conceal him from the enemy. She is not afraid to stand up to the men on both sides of the conflict (interestingly, it is only another woman who can effectively cross her plans). While not sacrificing any of her human weakness and vulnerability, she challenges boundaries of gender and class to assert her own desires and goals.

If Salomea forms the central point of the book's human action, at its symbolic center lies the river of the title. Yet, as with other natural elements in the book, the river is at once a symbolic element and a real actor. The river intervenes physically in the action at several points—hindering Odrowąż's escape from the Russians in the opening chapter, stopping Olbromski in his flight yet also safeguarding the precious documents he carries so they do not fall into Russian hands. Salomea returns to the river at the end of the novel, and here too it fulfills its role. The river might be said to represent both the hope and the despair that Żeromski perceives in the attempted rebellion. As with the uprising itself, what matters ultimately is not victory or defeat but faith.

Finally, it is worth saying something about the atmosphere of the novel. Żeromski's account of the uprising is broadly realist (for instance, in the historical details). He also has a penchant for naturalism in the style of Zola or Gorky—witness, for example, the blood-and-guts descriptions of Odrowąż's wounds, or his account of sexual relations, unusually frank for the time. Yet there is also a less realistic side to the novel. Żeromski's subtitle for the novel was *Klechda domowa,* which can be translated roughly as *A Fireside Yarn.* Elsewhere he described it as a tale "whispered on a dark night, through trembling lips, by those who were there, to children who shudder at the atrocities of a phantom." This perspective on *The Faithful River* highlights a certain Gothic quality in the writing and the plot, many elements of which were taken from actual stories about the uprising that Żeromski heard as a child. This is most clearly evidenced in the supernatural motif of the ghost of Dominik; yet throughout the novel it is important to remember that, rather than claiming to be writing a true historical account, Żeromski is offering us a personal, subjective tale that incorporates the distortions and exaggerations characteristic of events recalled at a distance or recounted at second hand.

The Faithful River, then, is both simple and complex. Its episodic plot masks a brilliantly direct, economical structure of narrative and character development. It can be read as a straightforward love story in time of war, and at this level it succeeds brilliantly. Yet it also works as an analysis of a crucial moment in Polish history by one who was barely born at the time, and who was writing from a perspective fifty years later. Finally, it is successful as a half-realistic, half-Gothic rendering of stories heard in childhood—partly recreating the world of those stories as it really was, and yet also partially acknowledging the fact that the stories themselves belong in the collective imagination as much as on the pages of a history book. It is this multilayered complexity that makes *The Faithful River* one of the greatest achievements of central European fiction in this century.

Bill Johnston

The Faithful River

I

The cold that tore at his innards had returned, and with it the pain that incessantly rent his head like an ax. His right hip ached ceaselessly, as if a metal fishhook were being pulled out from it. Every few moments an ineffable fire, unknown to a healthy body, ran across his back, while his eyes were blinded by a darkness filled with multicolored sparks. The wounded man bestirred himself and drew about him the short sheepskin jacket that, while it was still daylight, he had pulled off a dead Russian soldier in the undergrowth by the bank of the river. He thrust his bare legs and bloody hips deeper into the pile of corpses, in search of the two bodies that during the night had warmed him with the heat from their bleeding wounds, and with their howling and moaning had kept waking him from the sleep of death to the grace of life. But the two of them had fallen silent, grown cold, and become as hideous as the field covered in blood-spattered stubble. His arms and legs, seeking the warmth of those still alive, encountered nothing but wet, slippery cadavers.

He raised his head.

In his mind's eye he saw the events he had experienced; he saw the new deed through which his soul had suffered. Several hundred of them lay there, forming a white mound in the half-light of morning; they had been finished off as they lay wounded, at the order of the enemy commander in chief, a compatriot and not so long ago a fellow rebel. They had had the last shred of their clothing torn off them by the Russian soldiers, had been hacked to pieces by bayonets, pinned to the ground ten times over by the point of an officer's sword, run through, their heads blown apart by a bullet from a gun barrel pressed to their foreheads, crushed beneath the thundering wheels of Chengery's artillery.

The sandy soil was deep red from the blood, the last drop of which had run from these corpses. The hard clods of plowed earth had softened, the snow melted. Dragged there by the feet from all around, they had swept the broad field clean with their hair. They raked it with their stiffening fingers; they whispered their last words into the land, and tasted it as they wept their last tears.

The battlefield of Małogoszcz* was silent and dumb. The last living soldier looked upon it through the veil of half-death in the quiet morning twilight.

It seemed to him that only moments ago horses had stood on this spot. The earth still shook as three hundred comrades hurled themselves with a mortal cry upon the traitor! Where was his mount? Where was his broadsword? Where was the stirrup beneath his foot, his last companion?

The crash of Dobrowolski's grenades showering the valley could no longer be heard. The cossacks and dragoons on the flanks, who for over four hours had kept up a hail of bullets as they fired at will, were gone. Where there had been puffs and clouds of smoke and flashes of fire, the hill with its steep southern face lay gray in the silence. On the western side was the white strip of the cemetery wall where Jeziorański's men had had their stronghold, with their cavalry and cannon . . . And in the center, where the infantry had stood, there was nothing! Equipped with shotguns that could shoot barely a hundred paces—holding their fire—they stood under constant volleys from the enemy, who used them as target practice, armed as they were with rifles that had a range of fifteen hundred meters. They held their ground steadfastly, with the tenacity of Greek warriors—come and get us!—till the enemy should come within range, till the order to attack should ring out. Now they lay

*The Battle of Małogoszcz took place on February 24, 1863, in the Kielce region of central Poland.—TRANS.

piled in a single mound. In the distance smoke rose and drifted over the plain from the town, which the Russians had razed to the ground. At times a broad flame like the fluttering pennant of inexorability sprang up from the ashes, the billowing smoke, and the smoldering ruins, danced derisively in the gloom of death with its lambent brilliance, and spoke to the black sky with its ragged tongue. Then an anguished human cry burst from the charred rubble and reached the ears of the wounded man, whose heart was indifferent and who was unable to raise his hand. As with the fire in the ruins, feelings started up in the man, too; yet like that fire, in the black smoke of unseeing pain they were extinguished once more.

Sleet began to fall. Damp fog blew from the woods on the River Łośna. It stretched over the steep, bare hills, and trailed along the banks of the river and across the fields. It moistened his face like a wet cloth. In that morning mist a dark forest with its shaggy spruces could be seen. From the solid mass of trees it seemed that a breath of warmth wafted into the open ground: the gracious rustle of the branches. The long, wooden arms reached out and swayed slowly, sodden bundles of sticks spread low and calling in a hollow voice to run away from there.

There were no living people. No one, anywhere. Nearby lay a dead man who was dressed in coarse, dirty trousers. The injured man twisted across the field, pulled the trousers off, and hurriedly put them on his own naked, trembling legs. With his eyes he searched the corpses for boots, but not one of them had any. They had all been removed and taken as loot. All at once, from the east, by Bolmin, there came the boom of an artillery shell. After it a second . . . a third . . . That sound brought him to life. Something stirred in his entire being and revived his strength. A battle! To arms! To the ranks! He began to crawl on all fours in the direction of the noise, along a furrow, as fast as he could. But after a dozen yards or so he collapsed again, his head falling between the ridges of earth.

His right leg was trailing inertly. His hip was in agony. Feeling the place, with his middle finger he found a deep swollen hole from which blood was still oozing. He could not see out of his left eye. With his fingers he felt in the region of his brow, eyelid, eyeball, and cheekbone a protruding lump that throbbed and burned continuously, scattering colored flashes. His eye was no longer there; instead there was a great excrescence that was strange and ludicrous. From the sword cuts to his head during the battle, a great deal of blood had soaked into his hair; as it dried it had become matted and stuck together in tufts, creating a veritable red cap upon his skull. On his chest, across his ribs, and on his arms there was a multitude of suppurating bayonet wounds.

Yet stronger than any pain was the cold. It seized his bloodied hair in an iron fist, plunged its talons into his bones and between his ribs, and shook his shattered half-dead body with a merciless trembling. It was what drove him forward. Once again he set off on all fours. First on two hands and his left knee, then on his foot and hands, since his right leg dragged behind powerlessly; his whole figure turned into a truly laughable image of utter misery. In this way he crawled to the first trees of the forest. The spruce branches rocked in the winter rain and the fog. A wordless murmur fell from them to the ground. In it there was no pity, or compassion, or mercy, or contempt. For a long while that cold murmur drifted down to the man's dying heart.

The lone wanderer hoisted himself up on his hands, put his arms round the trunk of the first tree in the wood, and pulled himself up on his feet. He strained his ears, listening for the sounds of battle. Nothing broke the silence. He looked upon the battlefield. He was sorry neither for those who lay on the black field, nor for himself, nor for what had been done. Only one feeling dwelled in his breast, and only one thought remained beneath his blood-soaked hair: to fight. He had watched as soldier finished off wounded soldier, as they tore the clothes off the dying . . . There was nothing there with which he could extinguish a life that had turned into ignominy and absurdity. He missed the place where he had lain among the cadavers. He began to ask for death. He fell on his hands and face. His soul was overcome by darkness . . .

He lost consciousness for a long time, for when he awoke the sun was high. A sound of voices came from the field. He raised his head and saw people. They were dragging bodies somewhere up the hill. Someone was issuing orders to them. The wounded man was terrified that he would be buried alive. He began to flee. He crawled among the spruce thickets, through patches of half-melted snow, across slippery pine needles. His numbed legs warmed up from this movement, as he crawled on his hands and his knee. In his broken head the fugitive imagined that the wood was covering him up with its woolly greenery, that it was hiding him from evil eyes with a shaggy cowl; that someone unseen yet obviously present was ever so quickly pointing with a trembling hand to secret paths between the stumps that had been trodden by the fieldfares, trails made by the paws and tails of foxes.

In one place, deep in the woods on that labyrinthine route of his, in the heart of the forest, he came upon a crooked stick, a withered fir branch that had fallen from high up on the tree. At its thicker end this dry piece of wood had a knot that was just right for an armrest; and it was exactly the right length for a crutch. Leaning on this staff, for a second the fugitive wondered who had left it on an unused path for his injured leg. Was it almighty God—or merciless fate? And he laughed at their compassion; from the depths of his soul—which no longer desired anything, either from God or from fate, as it had experienced everything in the marches and battles of the uprising—he declared that he despised this compassion and that this proof of it he could cast away! But he reminded himself of his brothers in arms who had died, and of the smoldering field of Małogoszcz, and he gripped that last weapon tight at his side. What seemed like the vengeful cry of an eagle passed through his whole being, and a passionate force entered his heart. He felt within him the wild, mad, ancient soul of Czachowski,* made utterly pitiless by suffering. He moved forward, leaning on his stick, taking great strides, as if he were on stilts. It seemed to him that he was heading toward Bolmin, to the succor of his brothers.

From the movements of his body the pain in his hip, his back, and his head grew unbearable, like blows of a fiery rod. A veritable fire ignited in his bones and in his veins, spread to his head, and cast a veil of dark smoke over his eyes. Time and again his bare foot encountered in its path knots, roots, twigs, thorns, and needles hidden in the snow. The deep cuts bled. Several times his wounded body collapsed into the snow in some clump of bushes in the undergrowth or upon a sodden bed of moss. Chilled by the sudden cold, he started up again and blundered through the melting snow, amid bushes of frozen blueberries, working his way down the long, endless, meandering stretches of marsh that lay motionless upon the plain. As far as the eye could see and the ear could hear, the forest was empty. Here and there a woodland bird chirruped, startled by the rustle of human footsteps, and flew far away. The mute trees stood about with the mute sky above them; the earth had grown over with accursed plants that tormented the man's injured feet. Blood seeped out of his wounds. Traces of it marked the snow, the spruce branches, the bushes, and the moss.

*Czachowski was a Polish commander in the uprising known for his merciless treatment of the enemy.—TRANS.

To the eyes of the stumbling man the forest, which a short time before had been kindly toward him, was growing deeper, broader, and extending ever farther, revealing its bizarre pathways and inescapable mazes, its remote backwoods and loops, semicircular bends and unending corridors among trees. Hours had passed, and that immense forest was neither thinning out nor coming to an end. Here and there a sandy knoll rose up, as steep and difficult to climb as a mountain pass in the Tatras. The woodland path divided the expanse of trees into two parts and disappeared in between them. Leaning upon his crutch, the fugitive reached one of those windswept places. He lay down on it and decided to sleep there forever. Life and death had become undifferentiated and equal. All he wished for was to stop trembling with cold, to end his torment, and to stop thinking! He had forgotten which direction he was supposed to be heading in. He had lost his way.

He fell asleep at once. Yet it was a monstrous sleep filled with phantoms and hurly-burly. The forest about him seemed to shudder and groan. Everything in him was churning from the blows of his frenzied heart. In the depths of the earth on which his exhausted body lay, he dreamed there was the rumble of subterranean thunder and flashes of lightning. A cry of pain tore out from within and rent the sky asunder like a sword.

A violent trembling shook the fugitive once again and drove him onward. He resumed his crawling, his inert leg to the right side, his knotted staff to the left. He moved forward on his elbows and his knee, holding under his arm the crutch he had found. From the tails of his sheepskin jacket, spattered with mud and water, a loathsome cold penetrated his belly and chest, while its dry upper part soaked his bleeding wounds with perspiration. His feet, cut with thorns, swelled and left bloody traces in every puddle and patch of marshy ground. It was afternoon, for the sun was dipping down toward the treetops. A harsher chill swept across the forest floor. The wounded man searched for a place where he could burrow into the undergrowth and find shelter from the cold. But the ground was still sodden and covered with withered rushes. So he set off to the side, first one way, then the other, and made his way among prickly brush, brambles sprinkled with snow, osiers, and willows, bristling with outstretched thorns like the claws of a devil lying in wait. The slanting stalks of wild raspberry and hawthorn cut his face and tore at his hands.

He struggled through this wilderness, cursing his lot. When he had fought his way out of the scrub, he raised his eyes and, with profound astonishment, suddenly and unexpectedly saw a field—open ground—a low-lying meadow . . . It seemed as if God himself had drawn aside the hawthorns with his hand and allowed the man to look upon a treeless expanse. Snow-covered hills extended into the distance; at the foot of the farthest one he could see a row of cottages belonging to a village. Blue smoke rose from them into a sky flushed pink . . . At a distance from the village, broad buildings with stone columns and a manor house with a black roof were scattered among trees. This sight was so improbable for the soldier after the infinity of identical trees that it seemed to be an image from a dream, an illusion, an evil taunt . . . Homes . . . people . . . smoke rising from a cheerful fireplace . . .

The wretched man slumped to the ground. As he lay there, he looked powerlessly at the white clouds sailing across the lofty expanse of the heavens, at the inclined earth, at the human settlements. The last were as far away as the first. Nothing on earth or in the heavens wanted that sacrifice of wounds and spilled blood. Everything was turned against it. The earth on which his head had fallen was deaf; the open space was blind and dumb. A cold wind was blowing in from afar. Only that distant smoke . . . Blue, spiraling delightfully ever higher, it called like an incomprehensible yet benevolent summons.

The wounded man rested, then stood and, leaning on his stick, set off toward the village. This time the ground was even, without underbrush or thorns. The snow had melted somewhat during the day, then had been covered with a thin glaze of ice by the winter chill; this made his way easier. His legs moved along it smoothly and painlessly. Partly on all fours, partly using his crutch, he made his way across almost the entire width of the plain. From the village he could already hear the barking of dogs, the lowing of cattle, and human voices.

Yet between him and the edge of the pasture there appeared an unexpected obstacle: the river. Hidden amid high, rounded banks carpeted with ruddy grass, and twisting in countless semicircles that created an extended series of spits of land, the river flowed swift and black. On both sides it was frozen over at the banks, but there was no point at which the membrane of ice spanned the entire breadth of the river. The soldier crawled along the bank, searching for a sandbank or a footbridge by which he could cross to the other side. Nothing of the kind was to be found. Yet he was so drained of strength that it was impossible for him to continue to follow the turns of the river, which seemed to wind out of malice, as if to prolong his journey infinitely. Just like the forest before it, the river now constituted an impassable barrier. The line of the riverbank, which made his path into a zigzag, a weaving ribbon, was for the wounded man a new form taken by fate in its mockery of him. His injured legs rounded the spits, returning, it seemed to him, to the same place. A scoffing devil had cast this river down before him and set him dancing, cavorting left and right, without purpose and without end . . .

At one point, then, where the river flowed wider, the bank was less steep, and the water shallower, this Polish dancer interrupted his measure, slid down to the water's edge, and began to wade across. And the moment he entered the stream, he experienced a curious kind of relief. The black waters of the river reddened about him. The current in the center gurgled as if moaning from its very depths. With an immeasurably tender lapping, the water cleansed every wound assiduously and like a mother's lips kissed away the acute pain. The ancient and yet eternally new river absorbed into itself the liberally spilled blood of the insurgent, counting the drops, diligently soaking them up, taking them into its depths, dissolving them in itself, and carrying them far, far away . . .

The fugitive rinsed his swollen legs in the freezing water and, shaking from the fearful cold, climbed onto the bank. His coarse trousers clung to his legs and chilled him unbearably, but for decency's sake he left them on as he walked with his stick up toward the village. In this place the pastureland ended and the fenced-off fields began. Across the arable land a cattle track ran between the fences. This broad, sloping path, trampled by the hooves of the cattle and crisscrossed with deep ruts, was coated with frozen mud. The wounded man made his way along it with his last reserves of strength, holding on to the fenceposts and leaning on his stick. On this laborious journey, which seemed to him never-ending, he was met by people carrying pails down to the river for water. They were men and women, old folk and youngsters.

When they noticed him, they paused and stared at him curiously. Someone in the crowd hollered in the direction of the village, and someone else ran back hurriedly. The young insurgent walked on, slipping helplessly on the freezing mud.

The peasant farmers in their homespun coats and their sheepskin jackets began to appear from the direction of the village. Some of them approached at a stately pace; others were running and chattering among themselves. At the head of the crowd coming down the hill was a countryman with a yellow badge on his breast. He walked with a bold step and, standing close by, measured the bloody newcomer with his eyes. He asked:

"You there: Who are you?"

"You can see I'm a wounded man," came the answer.

"Where did you get wounded?"

"In battle."

"In battle? So you were in the uprising?"

"That's right."

"Well then, my friend, since you yourself say you're one of the rebels and that you were in the fighting, we're arresting you."

"Why?"

"We have to hand you over to the authorities in the town."

"You'd do that?"

"We sure would. Come with us. I'm the village councillor."

The red guest of the village was silent. These were the very people for whose freedom he had left a noble house and gone to sleep in the fields, in the winter, on the land; gone to starve, to obey orders like a dog, to fight without a weapon, and to return in this condition from the field of battle. They all came up and formed a semicircle around him.

Then he said:

"Let me go. I was fighting for your liberty; it was for your benefit that I received the wounds you see here."

"Yeah, we've heard those stories before . . . You can say what you like; there's been an order. Come of your own free will, my friend."

"Where do I have to go?"

"For the moment you'll come with us to the village. After that, you'll see."

"What are you planning to do with me?"

"We'll lay you down on the hay so you can get some rest. Then we'll line a cart with hay and drive you into town."

"You'd do that, too?"

"It's out of our hands. Orders are orders, that's all there is to it."

The wounded man said nothing and looked at them calmly. He shook with cold. He smiled ruefully at the thought that he had fought his way so arduously through the forest and across the river so that he could finally reach his goal . . .

Someone in the crowd called out:

"Come off it! Handing over this guy's just a waste of good horses. He won't even make it to the wayside shrine at Borek before he croaks."

"Did you see how his head's all covered in blood?"

"He musta stole that red cap from one of the farmers."

"He waded across the river. His sheepskin's dripping with water."

"Look, he's barefoot."

"Hey, Mr. Freedom, d'you lose your shoes?"

"Have you come far in this condition, soldier?"

"There's some kind of sign on his jacket."

"He probably stole it."

The councillor insisted, quarreling with his own as if he sought confirmation of his official actions from the whole crowd:

"Come on, fellers, we have to tie him up!"

"What, tie up this guy? . . ."

"It's a waste of cord!"

"We'll just get all dirty . . ."

"He's gonna die with or without rope."

"Let's just let him go," someone muttered.

"That's right. Let him crawl back where he came from."

"So long as he doesn't come into the village; if he's on the lane, it's none of our business."

"If it were some tough guy who's fighting and filling people with ideas, then of course you'd have to hand him over. But tying up an invalid like him . . ."

"After all, he's a Christian."

"Oh, right!" exclaimed the councillor. "They'll track him down, and they'll see how we had him in our hands and let him go . . . Then will you testify for me, wise guy, will you take a whipping for me?"

"Hey, I'm not the councillor. If we have to tie him up, then we just have to."

"We need some cord . . ."

"Someone go and fetch some cord."

"Let whoever's closest bring it."

"Get on with it!"

"I don't have any cord . . ."

"We can use string . . ."

"Sure; even birch twigs'll do fine . . ."

The wounded man noticed a gap in the rotten fence. He stepped sluggishly through the opening, leaning on his stick, and began to cross one strip field after another, at an angle, heading toward the buildings of the manor. He walked in that direction because that was where the opening led. The crowd followed after him, jabbering, deliberating, and arguing. Someone behind him was calling to him to turn back or to stay where he was. But since he didn't stay where he was, and the manor's outbuildings were close, the crowd of peasants grew less and less insistent. Instead loud volleys of laughter rang out at the sight of the fugitive's grotesque, ridiculous movements. Someone in the throng took a frozen clod of earth and hurled it. It hit the wounded man in the back. Someone else struck him on the head, causing it to droop even lower, toward the ground. They shouted various insults at him, but from ever farther away.

The young man limped behind the barn belonging to the manor and leaned his back against one of its stone columns. Through a burning fever that drew a film over his eyes, he could see the peasants standing at a distance and shaking their fists at him. He rested. He was out of the wind. It was quiet there in the corner between two walls, dry, wonderful. In his heart there was no sorrow, or regret, or the ashes of anything earthly.

Only the desire for eternal sleep.

So as not to have before his eyes the villagers, who had not dispersed but were still conferring in the field, he moved along the walls of the barn. Where the wall turned a right angle, he staggered on round the corner. He entered the courtyard. It was deserted. There wasn't a soul anywhere. The stables were wide open. The man looked inside but didn't see any horses. Snow had blown in and lay in drifts; the mangers, and the racks above them, were empty. On the far side of the courtyard stood the charred remains of buildings—cattle sheds, a granary, or another barn—that had been gutted by fire. Even the trees in the adjacent orchard were half-burned and the fences beyond them blackened with soot. Much lower, behind the ruins, could be seen the large, old-fashioned manor house.

The soldier crossed the yard and found himself at the kitchen entrance. Since the door was closed and there was no sign of movement anywhere, he gave a timid knock. Receiving no reply, after a long wait he took hold of the iron latch worn smooth with use and tried the door to see if it would open. It did. He entered a dark hallway full of kitchen utensils, empty tubs, pans, and baskets. To the left was a black doorway behind which noises could be heard. Once again he pressed down on the crude handle, opened the door, and stood on the threshold.

He was struck by the warmth of a fire that burned under the

kitchen range. How profoundly moved he was by that sight! Before the stove, facing the fire, there stood a tall, hunched old man with an extraordinarily thick shock of hair that was white as a dove; he was gazing upon a large cast-iron pot in which some kasha was bubbling as it cooked. The large manor kitchen was empty. At its far end was a shakedown bed with a dirty mattress. The newcomer called out, but the old man didn't look round. He called once more, again in vain. Then, reaching out with his stick, he tapped the other man lightly on the back.

The old fellow gave a start and spun round abruptly. He was exceedingly ancient, almost decrepit, but he was broad shouldered, rawboned, quick moving, and obviously strong. His face, which had the intense ruddy color of a winter apple, was a mass of countless wrinkles that crossed it in every direction like the marks left by a kitchen knife on a chopping board, creating veritable rays around his mouth and eyes. His luxuriant, thick, snow-white hair, above that furrowed countenance filled with power and a knowledge of life, glowed bright in the gloom. His great hands were like tools worn down and blunted by use. At the sight of the wounded soldier the old man's face grew stern and fierce. All the wrinkles gathered about his bushy eyebrows and his mouth, surrounding them like a forest of bristling needles.

"Get out!" he roared, stamping his feet in their great boots. His knees, poking out of holes in his sackcloth trousers, knocked furiously against one other. Between the open ends of the collar of his tattered sheepskin coat there could be seen a neck with folds of skin like a condor. Words were gurgling among those folds. His fists were clenched. Fury glinted in his eyes.

The intruder made no move to leave. He was looking greedily at the fire. To go out of this warmth into the cruel wind, in the wet rags that chilled his legs, to stumble once again across the frozen earth on his swollen feet . . . To see once again in his path that band of farmers . . .

In his heart he felt a profound happiness, a joyful peace; it was as if he heard a song being sung around his head. It occurred to him that he had paid all debts, he had redeemed not just his own sins, but those of others, too; and his soul felt good as never before in his life. He asked, with a gesture not of entreaty, but like a merchant's nod, whether he couldn't warm himself at the fire.

"Get out!" repeated the old fellow mercilessly. As he uttered the words over again, he fixed his small, piercing eyes, black as coals, upon the stranger.

"They'll burn down the manor because of you, you red devil! They've already fired the barns and the cattle sheds, you miserable villain! Get out this instant!"

The fugitive, incapable of crossing back over the threshold, sat down on it in his helplessness. His arms slipped to the ground; his crutch fell from his grip.

The old cook tugged his sheepskin about him and with his left hand felt for something in his breast pocket. He muttered to himself, baring his teeth, two of which were missing at the front. He suddenly bestirred himself. He seized hold of a clean bowl and, ladling out some kasha from the pot, tossed it in the bowl and handed it to the wounded man.

"Here, eat up and get out of here; otherwise they'll follow your trail. They'll burn down the manor and flog me to death. Come on, get on with it!"

The insurgent gestured to show he had nothing to eat with. The old man flung down on his lap an old, rough-edged wooden spoon. He scowled at the injured man as the latter lifted the scalding kasha to his mouth with trembling hands and swallowed it hurriedly and with indescribable relish, burning his lips as he ate. Soon the bowl was empty, and the delicious kasha was eaten to the last mouthful. The soldier indicated to the old man his legs—one distended at the hip, black and blue, the color of iron, the other with the foot scratched all to pieces, swollen and bloody. The old fellow bit his lip in disgust, cursed horribly, spat, and multiplied his insults; yet he studied the wounds.

Muttering to himself malevolently all the while, he shuffled over to his bunk, crawled beneath it, and, using a fire iron, pulled out a pair of worn-out red shoes—or, rather, the mud-bespattered uppers, soles, and heels from a peasant's hobnailed boots, made of stiff Russia leather, from which the tops had been torn off. The shoes were dry and hard, as if they were made of crude iron. The young gentleman put them on his feet, and clad now in these iron boots, he sat on the threshold. The cook looked him in the eye with the same severity as before and ordered him to leave the manor at once. Since the soldier lacked the strength to move, the old man seized him round the waist, picked him up, carried him to the hallway, pushed him out into the courtyard, and slammed the door behind him.

Now he had been driven out, the man wondered which way to go. He didn't want to head toward the farmyard because beyond it were the villagers. He was afraid to walk round to the front of the house, for it could be burned down on his account. Yet the road itself led him downhill, across the facade of the manor. It was a large stone building, elongated, with a double veranda and a large black roof. The road crossed in front of the verandas and continued down toward the river. The bloody soldier followed it.

He tried to pass the inhospitable house as quickly as possible. His feet hurt a hundred times worse in the heavy boots; he was weighed down by the stick in his hand, by the Muscovite sheepskin on his back, and, above all else, by that unbearable shame that he bore upon himself . . .

He walked by the first veranda without lifting his eyes. He was moving past the second . . . But someone called to him from that veranda. A young woman came down the few stone steps and, amazed at his fearful appearance, stood in the middle of the road. The wanderer raised his eyes to look at her, and despite his profound misery, staring through the mist of death, he was astonished and enchanted by her beauty. A piteous and at the same time joyful smile came to his lips. With no hat to take off, and unable to bow to this lovely figure, he simply gave a gesture of greeting with his hand. She looked upon him with dark eyes that surprise, curiosity, and a touch of pity rendered even more beautiful.

"Have you come from battle?" she whispered.

He nodded, smiling at her involuntarily.

"Where was it?"

"At Małogoszcz."

"Chengery was headed in that direction; he passed our way yesterday."

"That's right, though there were others, too."

She stepped closer, carefully examining his Russian army jacket.

"I'm an insurgent," he explained. "I took this from a Russian soldier on the battlefield, because they stripped us of our clothing."

"How did you find your way here?"

"Through the woods."

She looked at his red head, his injured eye, his legs running with blood; and she leaped into action, rapidly, briskly, all at once, and with a peculiar gaiety of spirit. She seized hold of his hand, pulled from it the knotted crutch, and cast the stick away over the broken remains of the garden fence. Then she took the wounded man by the arm and led him toward the steps of the veranda.

"They'll burn the manor," he said to her in a gentle voice, holding back reluctantly.

"We'll see about that; in the meantime, forward march when you're ordered!" she murmured hurriedly, helping him climb the steps.

With difficulty he hobbled up the steps and sat on a bench on the veranda. The young lady lit a lantern that stood there and opened the heavy door to the house, leading her guest behind her. His shoes clattered helplessly on the stone flags of the large, dark entrance hall. He climbed two more low steps and went through a doorway into a large room; led by the arm, he passed from one room to another.

Dusk was already falling in the manor. Immersed in a semidarkness illuminated only faintly by the light of the lantern, seen through the manifold fires of fever, this place seemed terrifying to the injured man. He imagined that death was upon him and that he was being led to some strange bedchamber by a beauteous angel of liberation. He wanted to turn back, to escape . . . but that small, strong hand did not let go. In this way he followed his guide through a large, cold, empty drawing room and was brought into a small heated chamber. The young woman sat him on a plain cretonne-covered couch and, leaving him alone, whispered, as if someone were eavesdropping:

"I'll just go and check whether anyone spotted us, and I'll clean the bloodstains from the veranda."

"An old man in the kitchen saw me."

"Oh, he's one of us. That's Szczepan, the cook."

"The villagers saw me heading for the manor."

"That's not so terrible, either. Anyway, you be quiet now . . ."

She left the room, taking the lantern with her. The injured man leaned back against the wall; it was only now that he felt the whole extent of his weakness. It was as if his sufferings had waited for this moment. They threw themselves upon him all at once, with their entire boundless force. He howled with pain . . . Through the film that covered his eyes, he saw the bright rectangle of the window, though in the room it was already dark. He saw the muslin curtains, the furniture; but his mind could not comprehend his good fortune, that his wounded body was beneath a roof, between the walls of a human dwelling. As in a dream, through his mind's eye there passed images of the battle, his escape, the forest, the river . . .

The door creaked. Quiet steps sounded. The young lady of the house came into the room, bearing her lantern. She put it on the table with a laugh and said:

"They've stolen everything from here, even the candlesticks. This lantern is all that's left. I have to sit by it as if I were in a cattle shed. Have you ever heard of such a thing? Anyway, I cleaned up the stains on the veranda. Are you feeling weak?"

"Yes; I have no strength."

"Where are you wounded?"

"In several places . . . I'll just rest for a moment. I'll be on my way soon."

"By all means, you'll be on your way soon. And where might you be headed, if I may ask?"

"Maybe somewhere round here there's a cellar or a woodshed or an attic where I could lie down in shelter. And wrap myself in something, a blanket or whatever, because I'm terribly cold."

"Just a moment . . ."

"I can go now, I'm already rested."

"Naturally . . ."

She left the lantern on the table and ran off somewhere. She was gone for quite some time.

The wounded man sank into an overpowering sleep, a dull, insensate dozing. Every other moment he stirred with the awareness that he must go at once, run away, hide; yet he lacked the strength to move his hand or nod his head. He lost track of how long this struggle with torpor lasted. But then the door opened and the old man who had been making the kasha appeared, helping the young lady to bring in a tub filled with water. Steam rose from the tub. After carrying it to the middle of the room, they set it on the floor. The old cook muttered noisily to himself, spitting and shrugging furiously, but the woman paid absolutely no attention to these manifestations of ill temper. He had to do what she ordered.

So she told him to bring soap, a sponge, a few sheets, towels, bandages, and lint. He fetched one thing after another, asking about each detail like a lady's maid and cursing each time he carried something in with the coarsest obscenities, as if it were he who were giving the orders. The woman shouted her instructions in his ear in an unfailingly cheerful tone. When the famulus had fetched everything that was needed, she instructed him to go to the kitchen and boil another kettle of water and to make sure that it was really piping hot. Muttering some fearful vulgarity, he left the room.

Then she pulled the thick, stinking sheepskin from the shoulders of the young man, who kept slipping helplessly out of her arms, and tossed it into the hallway. She took off the hard shoes, which were painful as leg irons, and threw them out, too. The soldier was almost naked now, dressed only in his wet trousers. With considerable difficulty she dragged him off the couch and onto a sheet spread out in the middle of the room, tipped his head over the rim of the tub, above the warm water inside, took the sponge, and began to moisten the dried spikes, lumps, and patches of blood in his hair. She rinsed out the hair with her small hands, separating it into narrow strands, carefully extracting one lock after another out of wounds caused by blows from sword and bayonet. Once she located the wounds themselves, she washed them solicitously and dried them with lint and old linen. Covering the cuts and scratches, she wrapped his whole head in a bandage, winding it skillfully crossways.

Soon the wounded man's head was properly dressed. But the tub was full of blood from the washing. The young nurse laid her patient on the ground and summoned the cook. When he came, scowling and snorting ominously, she shouted in his ear to begin by taking away the sheepskin jacket and the shoes, then to tear the sheepskin to shreds and burn it, and finally to fetch a fresh kettle of warm water. As soon as he had brought it, she sent him for a pail for the bloodied water in the tub. He had to do everything quickly and nimbly, because otherwise she frowned and stamped her foot. He took the dirty water outside and emptied it onto the compost heap.

Meanwhile, the young lady poured the clean water into the tub and set about dressing the man's cheek. Here her task was infinitely more difficult than with the cuts on his head. It was hard to know whether the eye had survived, because beneath the eyebrow, half of his face was covered with a single black swelling covered with dried blood from the wound. For the longest while the youthful physician shone her lantern at this eye and examined its condition by the light of the tallow candle. Her lovely fingers searched for the position of the wound, feeling for the eyelid and the eyeball. She concluded that this was not an injury from a bullet or a sword, but that he had been stabbed in the eye with a bayonet. The blade had struck against the cheekbone and slid across it toward the nose, tearing the skin and prising the eyeball from its socket. It was impossible to tell whether the eye was whole, or even whether it was still there.

She set about splashing water onto the laceration and cleaning it out. She covered the open wound with lint, wrapped the place with a bandage, and moved on to the bayonet cuts on the arms and between the ribs. These were mostly contusions and shallow scratches. On the man's back she found cuts from a sword, the force of which had been lessened by his fur jacket and his shirt.

The most serious and dangerous wound was the one in his hip. The young doctor had to set aside her modesty and remove what was left of the man's clothing. When she touched the hip wound, which was greatly swollen, the soldier shrieked with pain. It was clear that this was no mere bayonet cut or external injury, but that a bullet was lodged deep within. In vain she tried to feel for the bottom of the wound with her fingers and find the bullet. It was wedged deep down among the bones, veins, and sinews, since it caused the man agony with every movement. She had to be content with cleaning and bandaging the wound. The washing of the man's feet, from which she removed all the thorns and splinters, completed her ministrations.

After dressing the injured soldier in a man's shirt that she found in the wardrobe, she wrapped this collection of wounds in a clean sheet. Then, with great difficulty, as if she were struggling with something that weighed as much as a young colt, after some lengthy maneuverings she hauled the helpless man into her own maidenly bed. She covered him conscientiously with a blue satin quilt on top of a thin sheet and set about carefully scrubbing the bloody stains on the floor, pouring the red water into the pail, carrying it all out with the aid of the cook, and generally tidying up the whole room.

Her guest was conscious. He did not fall asleep. He watched the beautiful woman bustling about the room. He gazed at her head, which was handsome in every pose and from every angle, with its raven-black hair parted in the center and clinging to her temples; at her regular features, imbued with an indescribable charm; at her rose-colored lips, on which a radiant smile was forever to be seen . . . She wore a dress broad at the bottom, as the fashion was, yet without the dimensions of a crinoline. Her cheeks were flushed from her labors, and her hands were smeared with blood. Watching this unknown and yet so enchanting being, who had washed his most personal essence, his wounds, and his disgusting filth with a joyful naturalness and a simple goodness, he choked on tears of happiness. God had sent him that happiness after his great suffering. As he had been cursing and blundering through the forest and across the water, it had been waiting for him in this house. He, he alone, had been called to it . . .

He recalled the naked corpses piled up in the fields—the bodies of valiant men, dragged by the heels to the pit beyond the woods—and he immersed himself in God . . .

Phantoms and torments, fearsome specters and unimaginable voices, beset him on every side. Grotesque apparitions bent over him, taking the form of trees, or of foam-flecked animals that galloped over his head in a rumble of hooves. His arms were heavy, as if made of marble. His hands were suspended somewhere high overhead, as if attached to the ceiling; then they felt so small, he couldn't find them by his side. His legs were tossed about like tree trunks in a sawmill. His head seemed like a heated anvil upon which, right by his ear, a host of strongmen were striking with their hammers.

II

The sun shone magically. Fiery whirls shimmered upon the pine floorboards, which had been washed clean of the stains from the day before and were by now dry. Something seemed to be merry, laughing from happiness, hovering about the place where the tub had stood, twinkling now brighter, now dimmer. The injured man stared at the patches of light and reveled in the sight. The young lady of the house came in. In her hands she bore a steaming bowl of food and a silver spoon. She stared hard at her patient. Seeing that he was not asleep, she smiled like a gleeful rapscallion in school and with her eyes gave an amusing sign of complicity. She nodded to him, saying:

"You see, sir, the night's passed, it's midday, and you've not died."

"Really?"

"Of course! In a moment you'll be eating kasha; I think that's proof enough!"

"Kasha? Like I had yesterday?"

"Yes."

"That's wonderful!"

"Exactly, that's what I thought, too. All the more so because there's nothing else Szczepan and I have to offer you. Please forgive us, then, but what's ours is yours, and so on . . . I mean, if we only had a handful of flour, a pinch of sugar, a little milk. Not a chance! Nothing but kasha and more kasha. Even chickens would be sick of it, don't you agree?"

"Not for the moment, at least. Insurgents don't get sick of things even when the chickens refuse to peck at them. I just hope it isn't as hot as it was yesterday."

"It's not at all hot. Besides, I can easily cool it down, because there's a quite a frost today. But perhaps you don't even care for kasha?"

"Far from it! Like I said, in our unit we were always having kasha, sometimes a few potatoes . . . It's just that yesterday I burned my mouth on it."

"My, what a martyr you are! You're all cut to pieces, and stabbed, and shot, and on top of everything you've burned your mouth. That's the last straw."

"I'm sorry, miss."

"There's no need to apologize. Some things one grows so used to, they become second nature. As far as the kasha is concerned, I should tell you we have nothing but that sack of barley. And that's a secret! A secret, sir! If they sniff that out and take it away, there'll be hungry times."

"And where does your household keep this sack?"

"'Household'! There's no household, only Szczepan, the old cook you met. He hides it in the hayloft in the barn. He's made a hole in the hay several feet deep; he drops the sack down into it on a cord every morning at dawn, as soon as he's taken out a portion for the two of us."

"Excuse me, miss, but where am I? What's the name of this place?"

"You don't even know that?"

"No. I'm a stranger here, this is the first time I've been in these parts."

"This is Niezdoły Manor. It belongs to Mr. and Mrs. Rudecki, my relatives and guardians."

"And you, miss? Forgive me for asking . . ."

She smiled gaily and most attractively and said:

"My name is Salomea. But don't imagine that I'm one of the

local Jews. My family name is Brynicka; I'm related to the Brynickis who used to own Mieranowice. That was my father's uncle and his wife. Mrs. Rudecka is my aunt; she's not a blood relation, but family is family."

"I didn't imagine anything of the sort! It's a lovely name."

"Oh, yes indeed!" She nodded with a bitter note of pity. "No one can get over the fact that a name like that can be given to a human being. Salusia, Salcia . . . Good Lord! 'Saltsche,' in Yiddish . . ."

"Salce in Italian means 'willow.' It's a beautiful tree and a beautiful name."

"In Italian? You speak Italian?"

"I know a little, though not a great deal; enough to hold a conversation. I learned, I hardly know when myself, while I was in Italy."

"You've been in Italy? Oh my . . ."

"Why do you sigh like that?"

"Oh, just from envy. It must be wonderful to be in Italy, 'beneath an Italian sky.' . . . Is the sky really special there?"

"It's the same as here."

The wounded man narrowed his eyes; he was seized once again by wrenching pains and a burning fever. He stared into space with a glazed expression. After a while he regained control of himself, came to, and said:

"You have no idea who I am, yet you gave up your bed for me . . ."

"I know you're an insurgent."

"My family name is Odrowąż, and I was christened Józef."

After a moment he added: "You know, miss, from my parents I inherited the title of duke . . ."

"Duke?" whispered Miss Salomea, studying him half in disbelief, half in awe. Her face grew graver and her movements more cautious. Yet it didn't last long.

"I have a sizable estate," he added. "And yesterday . . ."

"Oh, yesterday you gave the game away, not so much with your riding boots, because they were ever so slightly topless, as with your aristocratic sheepskin jacket." She smiled teasingly.

The sick man closed his eyes in embarrassment. Everything was churning within him. He spoke slowly.

"I'll try . . . right away . . . as soon as . . . I'll be up and heading back to my unit, so as not to expose you to any unpleasantness . . ."

"Oh, you and your threats! Your Grace would do better to stop talking and rest quietly. I don't mind telling you that this was the first time in a long while, in four weeks or so, that I got a good night's sleep in your care."

"Well, I never! In my care?"

"Certainly. You ought to know, Your Grace, that in the entire house there's no one but the old cook, Szczepan, who's deaf as a willow post—*salce* in Italian—and myself, also 'Saltsche.'"

"So where is everyone?"

"Where are they? Gone. Mr. Rudecki, my uncle, was put in prison two months ago. The Rudeckis had five sons. Julian, Ksawery, and Gustaw joined the insurgents right away, the first two from home, and Gucio directly from school in Puławy. The two youngest boys are at school in Kraków. Julian died in battle somewhere near Miechów; while poor Gucio . . ."

Miss Salomea wept bitterly. After a while she wiped her eyes and said: "Ksawery perished, too. My aunt, the boys' mother, went to search the prisoner-of-war camps. It's been four weeks since she left. One of the local Jews, the innkeeper, who trades in horses, or rather steals them, saw my aunt as she was on her way back from somewhere in the Sandomierz district. Then later there was a rumor among the farmers hereabouts, who've recently taken to catching insurgents and handing them over to Chengery, that she was trying to secure the release of my uncle from prison in Opoczno. Apparently she found Ksawery's body in a barn."

"Where does this news come from?"

"From Skowron, the driver who was traveling with my aunt. They left in a four-horse carriage, but the driver returned alone and on foot. My aunt had had to sell the horses, the carriage, too, because she needed the money to bribe them to set Uncle free. When the driver came back, he didn't even call in to tell us what had happened, but instead he went directly to his village. We heard what he said at fourth hand."

"And what did he say?"

"It seems that all those who had been killed were dressed in long sackcloth shirts down to their feet, and at their neck every one of them wore a tricolored cockade. And they were all lined up in a row before being buried. And Ksawery was among them."

"Shirts, cockades! How splendid, how gracious!" Odrowąż laughed. He turned his face upward and stared at the ceiling.

Miss Salomea continued:

"And just imagine what happened to Gucio. During one of the battles he fled on horseback. He found his way onto a lane near some village, and he would have gotten away, because he was riding a magnificent horse, a chestnut that had been reared from a foal on our pasture. As luck would have it, a calf wandered into the middle of the road and the chestnut ran into it. The dragoons who were chasing Gucio caught up with him. They set about him with their sabers, hacking and slashing till there was nothing but a headless, armless cadaver for the horse to carry off across the fields. Apparently the runaway creature carried the body on its back for miles and miles, then dragged it even farther when it fell from the saddle and one foot was caught in the stirrup. That horse! Who would have thought it . . . We all loved him, we used to adore riding him bareback or in the saddle. How could he have had such an accident, not jump over the calf, betray his young master! Darling Gucio! He was so handsome, so cheerful . . ."

She gave a sob and cried a short while. Odrowąż was silent, without compassion as he watched her tears. She wiped her eyes and added:

"All the servants have left the house. One night the insurgents under Jeziorański came here, and the Russians followed soon after. The rebels barricaded themselves in the distillery and the granary and began firing from the windows and the vents. The Russian soldiers set the granary on fire. The roof of the distillery caught fire, too. Everything burned to the ground: the distillery, the granary, the cattle sheds, and the barns. At least we were fortunate that the wind blew the smoke out onto the meadows, because the other barn wouldn't have survived, nor the stables, nor even the manor—that's how big the blaze was. Since then everything's gone from the house. They took every last horse, while someone stole the foals in the night. And since the time my father left to join the uprising, only Szczepan and I are left."

"Then your father's still alive?"

"He is. My father has worked as my uncle and aunt's steward here at Niezdoły for twenty-two years, ever since he returned from Siberia. Because in the last revolution* he was a sergeant major in the light horse, and for that he was exiled to Siberia."

"Is your mother still alive?"

"My mother died when I was one, twenty-two years ago. No, twenty-one . . ."

"I see you're taking a little off your age."

"Are you saying I should add to it? I'm not taking anything off."

*Referred to here is the November Uprising of 1830–31 against the czar.—TRANS.

After a moment she added with something like pride and something like embarrassment, the way one talks of family matters and details that are important and meaningful only in one's own circle and have no significance for outsiders:

"My father has only six fingers on both hands together."

"How's that?"

"The others were blown off by a musket ball at the battle of Długosiodło, just as he was holding his carbine to his cheek and taking aim. He lost two fingers here and two here. It's so funny when he washes . . ."

She demonstrated, placing her hands together.

"And your father left you all alone like this?"

"Oh yes, because the first duty of a Pole is to his fatherland, and only then to his family." She uttered this wise and conventional popular dictum with hieratic solemnity.

"And how do you manage when the soldiers come? Do they come?"

"I should say! We're lucky to have a night without them. And when it's not the Russian army it's our own. And the moment ours leave, the Russians come back."

"And you're always alone?"

"Well, Szczepan's here."

"The old fellow?"

"He may be old, but he's wise and cunning as a fox; whatever happens he knows what to do, and his peasant tricks always work. And let me tell you something else, Your Grace: He's not afraid. Or at least, he is afraid, because sometimes he quivers like calves' feet in jelly, but he'd never run away. If the time came when he had to stand his ground—and he alone knows when that might be—he would never let me down, and he'd take everything upon himself. They've thrown him out a hundred times, and he always creeps back in, listening and waiting. The moment I call, he's by my side. If I were attacked, he would defend me at any cost. He can be depended on. Besides, if worst comes to worst, I have another protector here."

"Where?"

"Here," she declared with a smile, pulling a double-barreled pistol from the pocket of her broad dress.

"Who on earth gave you that?" asked Odrowąż.

"Father."

"And that was the only protection he left you with?"

"Father said that I should use it only at the very last minute, if someone were attacking me by force. And above all he told me to defend myself till the very last moment with the honor of a Polish woman."

"With the honor of a Polish woman . . ."

"You think that has no meaning, Your Grace? I've seen what it means a number of times here. And I'll tell you one more secret that'll set your mind at rest. I have an accomplice. But it mustn't get out, because without her we'd be in a sorry way."

"My lips are sealed."

"In that case I'll tell you. There's an inn hereabouts that stands in open country at a crossroads about a quarter of a mile from the manor. The inn is owned by some Jews. At one time they used to buy vodka from the manor, while the distillery was still in operation. Now they get it from somewhere else, and do whatever work comes to hand, which is mostly smuggling stolen horses out of the area. That's what the word is. I can't say for sure myself. Actually, no one will ever know the whole truth, because it's all put down to the uprising. There are horses at the inn, then they disappear. Supposedly it's the insurgents who take them . . . There are a whole number of Jews living at the inn. But among them there's a child of maybe fourteen or fifteen. Her name's Ryfka. You should see that little scarecrow by the light of day. She hasn't washed in four years or more; her hair is all matted, and she's dressed in filthy rags."

"Sounds like me yesterday."

"Even worse, though at least she isn't covered in blood. When Siapsia, the old innkeeper, was contracted to look after the cows from the manor herd, Ryfka would come here at dawn to milk them and measure out the milk. I used to have to get up before dawn too to tend the cows. So out of boredom the two of us would talk about this and that. Once in a while I'd give her something or other. And sometimes I'd call for her at the inn on a summer's evening and we'd slip away at night through the mist down to the river, where we'd run barefoot through the unmown grass covered in dew . . . Your Grace will be shocked that I compromised myself with a little Jewish girl . . ."

"Nothing could be further from my mind!"

"I didn't entirely take her into my confidence, but she knew how to keep a secret; she was faithful, and she stuck to me like a shadow. At other times we arranged to go pick the wild raspberries and blackberries that grow on the hill in back of Niezdoły. She went everywhere with me and listened to what I had to say. Whatever I did she copied me; if I changed something, so did she. Whatever I liked she did, too. If I didn't like the taste of something, she'd pull a face. When I sang to myself, she'd sing along with me, word for word, note for note, and she was so funny, you could split your sides laughing. I had to put my hand over my mouth so as not to hurt her feelings. Sometimes I would sing some utter nonsense, or make up silly songs for her to learn.

"Anyway, Ryfka became my friend. But a true friend. Now, when the soldiers appear in the night, wherever they're coming from or going to they pass by the inn, because the inn stands at the crossroads. And if they only ask the way to Niezdoły manor, Ryfka creeps out the back door, through the recesses and corners, passageways and outbuildings, past trash cans and manure heaps, then over the wild hill, across the gully, through the garden to me. If it's the insurgents who are on their way to the manor, she knocks on the window, on that pane there, three times. If it's the Russians, four times. Then I go down to the kitchen, wake Szczepan, and in the dark the two of us prepare ourselves and wait. Only when they begin rattling the windows and hammering at the door with their rifle butts does Szczepan go and let them in. But by then we at least have some idea what to do. Do you understand, Your Grace?"

"I do, though my leg is very painful. But as far as my title is concerned, we'll always know that it's there and will never go away, so there's no need to remind ourselves constantly of it."

"Your Grace is something of a, what's the word, a democrat . . ."

"You could put it like that."

"In that case we shall speak plainly with each other. The point is that now you're here, Ryfka has really become important. Don't you agree?"

"Oh, yes."

"Because each time they come they search the entire house, not excluding my bed. They poke around everywhere. Sometimes one of them gets embarrassed and orders his men just to cast their eyes about. But there are others who deliberately, mockingly, go rooting around in every nook and cranny."

"What can we do when they come?"

"When Ryfka knocks we'll know who's coming. And if she knocks four times, Szczepan will have to pick you up and carry you out of the house. I think the barn would be best."

"That will be terribly difficult."

"Not really. The old man can manage. Even your noble title will help, because Szczepan can have it explained to him that you really are a rich aristocrat."

"I'm not sure about rich, but my family will reward him abundantly."

"There you are. *Ça ira*!"

"You don't know Italian, but you speak French."

"Well, yes, I learned at boarding school, at the convent in Ibramowice. I didn't actually graduate, because Father ordered me to come back and help with the household. Though to tell the truth, I wasn't exactly wild about school. But I've been chatting on and on and you've not had anything to eat. I'll heat up some fresh kasha; the old bowl has gotten cold and gluey. Szczepan may even have a drop of milk from the Jews; though it's only goat's milk," she added embarrassedly.

With that she left the room.

Upon her return she found her guest plunged into a sudden, febrile sleep. She tiptoed closer and examined his bandages. Here and there blood had soaked through the cloth. In a number of places the pillow and sheets were marked. She was sorry for the sheets, but also a little for this lanky fellow who called himself a duke. She was sorry that his regular features, his straight nose with its magnificent profile, and his handsome head should have been so disfigured by his wounds. She sat quietly in the corner of the room, sighing at the course events had taken, till the man woke up. Then she forced him to eat a few spoonfuls of kasha, without the promised milk, but warm nevertheless. He begged her pardon over and again for the inconvenience she was suffering on his account. The constant repetition of this apology roused her indignation. To put an end to it once and for all, she declared:

"I already told Your Grace it's only now, under your protection, that I can breathe more easily."

"It's all very well to joke . . ."

"It's no joke! If you knew just what goes on here at night, you'd understand what I'm talking about."

"Whatever can it be that goes on here?"

"It's not so easy to explain!"

"You mean about the soldiers coming?"

"There's that, too. But also . . ."

"What is it?"

"You saw how big this house is?"

"I caught a glimpse of it, but yesterday it was hard for me to notice anything in detail."

"It has eighteen rooms. Some large, some small. There are three drawing rooms alone. One of them, the biggest, stretches across the entire width of the building in the stone-built part at the back. And there's only me to look after it all."

"Are you afraid?"

"It's easy for you not to be afraid, you're a man. Besides, you don't know the whole story."

"And what else ought I to know in order to be properly afraid?"

"You see, there's a certain matter," she said, pulling her chair up to the bed and dropping her voice to a whisper.

"A long time ago, after the revolution, the two Rudecki brothers lived here. They shared the management of the property, because there were nine farms, the distillery, sawmills, a stud farm, cattle—in a word, a considerable estate. The older brother, Dominik, who later passed away, had previously served in the army. I have to tell you that he had also been in love with my aunt, before she married Uncle Paweł, the one who's still alive and is now in prison.

"My late uncle Dominik was responsible for the distillery, the horses, the mills, the woods, and the sawmill: all the manufacturing side. Uncle Paweł oversaw the farms. And they lived like this together. Uncle Dominik was always at the far end of the manor, on his own, because he and Uncle Paweł were forever arguing over money and everything else. Uncle Dominik took his meals alone in his part of the house. His dinners were sent over there. My father once told another man who'd also been in the previous revolution that Uncle Dominik had always been in love with my aunt and bore a huge grudge against his brother for having won her. It was apparently because of this that he began to behave eccentrically. He occupied himself exclusively with his horses, dogs, greyhounds, and bloodhounds. He spent all his time hunting or target shooting with shotgun and pistol.

"Once he and Uncle Paweł fell out over the distillery. It seems that Uncle Paweł had evidence to show that the distillery wasn't doing well and was producing little income, and that because of the distillery the farms were going downhill. So then Uncle Dominik closed the distillery and boarded it up, laid off the workers, and ordered all the containers, the great barrels and the vats hooped with iron bands, to be brought from the distillery to the biggest drawing room next to his own room, where he had them placed all in a row. The furniture was removed from the drawing room, and the distillery was turned into a woodshed. To this day all those vats are standing in the great drawing room. Then, one evening, just imagine it, in the last room beyond the drawing room where he lived, Uncle Dominik tied a loaded shotgun to the door, sat with the barrel pointing at himself, and pushed on the trigger with his foot. He killed himself."

"Was this long ago?"

"About ten years back. I was in the convent at the time. But let me tell you, that was only the beginning!"

"His death?"

"That's right. Uncle Dominik was mourned; they put up a

tombstone in the local church cemetery and had masses said for his soul. And then . . ."

"What is it? What are you so afraid of?"

"He still walks about the house . . ."

"What on earth do you mean?"

"I mean just that, and everyone else says so, too. The entire neighborhood knows about it."

"We should be laughing at the very idea!"

"You can laugh when you've heard him."

"What can I expect to hear?"

"Anyone who's been here will tell you what he gets up to. Just listen. He takes those huge vats, in their iron bands, lifts them up as if they were single-gallon kegs, and hurls them from high up by the ceiling onto the floor. The vat bounces off the floor once, twice, three, four times. You can hear it clear as anything: bang—bang—bang—bang! Then the same with another vat. And a third. And he repeats this ten or fifteen times."

"Very well, but did anyone go and watch him doing it?"

"Of course! They took candles and went with the servants, the whole manor together. They took the village priest and a holy monk from the Miechów region. Every one of them heard him flinging down the vats; the whole crowd went there with candles and entered the great drawing room. The vats were standing in a row, lined up, as they had been before. From one to the other stretched spiders' webs that had been there since goodness knows when and were covered with a thick layer of dust as they had been for years."

"You see, then, it must have been an illusion."

"An illusion! Everyone who spends the night here begins by saying the same as you and ends up trembling in fear. The priests even blessed the vats."

"And you've heard him?"

"How could I not have? Twenty times or more. Sometimes, when he sets to, the whole house quakes. But as if that were all! He walks around the house! Everyone's seen him. In a tobacco-brown riding coat with horn buttons and close-fitting britches with ankle straps. Once at dusk he passed by my aunt so close that the horn buttons on the back of his coat clearly, ever so clearly, brushed against the slatted edge of the bookcase. My aunt fainted."

"I'd like to believe it, because you're the one telling me; but I can't."

"In that case I'll tell you the best part. My aunt and uncle gave a lot of money to the priests so that they would keep saying masses for Uncle Dominik's soul. The parish priest, who's an elderly man and a wise cleric, told us this story himself, and his hands shook in terror. He said that he and the curate had been sitting together one evening in the main room of the presbytery, discussing which masses they had to say the following day. And since there had been a great number of votive offerings, though there was supposed to be a mass for Uncle Dominik they decided to postpone it till another time. And the priest confessed that he and the curate committed a sin, because they talked about how so many masses had been said for the suicide, while there were other souls who also needed help. Besides, the priest observed, this time the Rudeckis had either forgotten, or neglected, to offer something for the mass. And so he and the curate thought about not saying mass for Dominik the next day, but putting it off till later instead.

"The curate took his quill and was about to write in the register the names of those for whom mass would be said. There wasn't a living soul in the room other than the two men. When the curate had written the first letter of some name, a gold ducat dropped loudly onto the table as if it had fallen from the ceiling; it spun round between the two clerics and came to rest in the light of the candle between their hands. That was how he was paying them, in his own way, scoffingly. The priest told us that they were both terrified. They immediately took the ducat to the church, put it on the altar as a votive offering, and prostrated themselves beneath the lamps, in the night, praying fervently for Dominik's soul. The next day the two of them said requiem masses."

"Strange things . . . And while you've been here alone, have you seen any ghosts?"

"No. For some reason things have calmed down of late. He's not been throwing the vats around and banging the way he usually does. There was only one time, but I won't speak of that."

"There's no need. Try to forget it."

"But just think. The soldiers come here; they search the house, shouting, making a racket, and frightening me. Then, when at last they go away and I ought to be able to breathe more easily, I'm left on my own and I start to be afraid of him. Now that you've come I'm not in the least scared. That is, I am, but only of the soldiers. And at least with them one's dealing with human beings . . ."

"Human beings? Really?"

"You can defend yourself, fight them tooth and nail, even die; whereas with him—!"

"You weren't afraid today?"

"Not in the slightest! I slept like a log, even though I'm a very light sleeper and when Ryfka knocks I hear it straight away."

"And where are you sleeping?"

Miss Salomea grew embarrassed and turned bright red, saying: "I'm sleeping there in the other room."

"Where?"

"In the drawing room."

"In that cold place?"

"I pulled my mattress up near your door, where it was warm from this room; and I slept there. Because, you understand, I have to be near the window in case Ryfka comes and knocks."

III

Foreseeing nothing but disastrous consequences if the wounded man were to be found in the house, Miss Salomea was obliged to look for a hiding place for her patient. After lengthy discussions with Szczepan, a safe location was agreed upon. Along with the stables, a barn that stood somewhat apart had survived the burning of the outhouses. It contained hay left after the destruction or theft of all the rest of the family's property. One partition of this barn was piled with hay right up to the roof trusses. It was here that Szczepan hid his sack of kasha. And it was here that he decided also to conceal the insurgent if the need arose.

In the center of the partition, starting from the top, he dug out a kind of well in the hay, about ten or twelve feet deep. The hay had settled in the autumn and winter and was packed tight underneath, so the walls of the shaft were solid and kept their shape just like a real well casing. Right at the bottom, he drilled a kind of funnel leading to the outside wall of the partition, so the soldier would be able to breathe. Among the ruins of the distillery he found an ancient door with metal fittings; its corners had been burned in the fire, and it had acquired an oval shape. He used this door as a lid to cover the well, first hollowing out a frame of the right size in the hay. On top of the door he placed a further layer of straw, so the hiding place was completely concealed. At the same time, they thought about how the injured man should be clothed. In the wardrobes they found Mr. Rudecki's long, thick bearskin traveling coat and a pair of fur-lined boots. These were kept on hand, along with two new long straps.

To begin with, Miss Salomea slept in the cold drawing room

adjoining her former bedroom, now occupied by the wounded man. But she was afraid that she would sleep through the warning knock on the window, so she was forced to leave the bedroom door open. Furthermore, the unheated drawing room was unbearably cold; sleeping on a mattress laid out on the floor was a real hardship for her. There was no way that the room could be heated: Szczepan had long been chopping up the fences from the kitchen garden and the whole courtyard, and there was barely enough wood for the kitchen range and the stove in the bedroom. There was nothing for it . . . Miss Salomea, whom everyone in the family called Mija, had to start spending her nights in her old room, now the duke's bedchamber. Here, on the little couch, only half undressing, she covered herself with the bearskin coat and dozed by the injured man. Every evening, when it came time to retire, she burned with embarrassment and was stifled by the worry that someone would get the wrong idea. The fear that this man's presence in the house would be revealed forced her to overcome her discomfort.

The third night she sat half-asleep by the sick man, who was raving in a fever, moaning and groaning. Suddenly there were four knocks on the window. Then came four more. The knocks were loud and hurried. Miss Mija leaped to her feet in an instant; she ran across the hallway that separated the bedroom from the kitchen and woke the cook. The old man rushed in at once, muttering in his usual way. She shouted in his ear that they were coming and set about hastily dressing Odrową ż. They pulled some thick trousers on his legs and wrapped him in the bearskin coat; then they slipped loops of the straps under his arms and around his knees, and the strong old man steadied himself to pick up the load as if it were a sack of corn. Miss Mija arranged the burden on his back, unlocked the door from the hallway to the back garden, and closed it behind him.

Szczepan waded uphill through the snow, gasping and grunting under the huge weight. He reached the barn, and from a side entrance he had prepared earlier he clambered up the hay in the partition to the very top. He felt for the wooden lid of the hiding place and, ordering the duke to remain deadly silent, went to work. He moved aside the lid, took the ends of the straps in his hands, and set about gingerly lowering the wounded man into the black opening. Once he was on the bottom, the old man tied the ends of both ropes to a staple that was still fastened to the door, closed the top of the hole, and scattered hay over the lid. He carefully smoothed over the hay, slid quickly back down, locked the barn, and hurried back to the manor.

He slipped through the darkened kitchen and the hallway and stopped in the bedroom. His first thought was to change the sheets on the soldier's bed. Miss Mija was already working on it. The pillow had bloodstains in a number of places from the man's wounds, which were still bleeding and kept soaking through the unskillfully applied bandages. It was the same with the blanket and the mattress. Together the two of them hastily changed the pillowcases and laid down clean sheets.

They were just finishing when from outside there came the sound of horses' hooves and the tramping of large numbers of feet marching in step; then voices were heard surrounding the manor on all sides. All at once blows rang out on the doors on both verandas; rifle butts hammered on the shutters, and there were loud shouts for them to open up. Szczepan did not obey at once. First he carried the bloodied pillowcases and sheets to the unlighted kitchen and hid them in some inaccessible hiding hole in the bread oven where the devil himself wouldn't have been able to find them. Only when the banging on all the doors and shutters was so violent that it sounded as if they would be torn off their hinges did he go to the front veranda and open the main door. He was immediately rewarded for his pains. Miss Salomea lit a lamp and waited in the cold drawing room.

The door was flung open and a whole group of officers poured into the room. They were wearing kepis over which hoods were tied, thick boots, and winter greatcoats on which the straps of their sabers and knapsacks glistened. They were led by their commanding officer, an older man with a gray mustache and sideburns. The officers entered the large room, walked up to Miss Salomea, and surrounded her. The older man asked in broken Polish:

"Who are you?"

"A relative of the owners of this manor."

"Where are the owners?"

"Mr. Rudecki, my guardian, is in the city, in prison, I believe, and his wife has gone to try to secure his release."

"Where are their sons?"

"Some of them are in school . . ."

"Where would that be? Which schools?"

"In Kraków."

"And the others?"

"The others have all left; I don't know where they are."

"You say you don't know where they are?"

"No."

"And what's your name?"

"Salomea Brynicka."

"It was your father who was the steward here?"

"That's right."

"Where is he?"

"He's gone away."

"Where did he 'go away' to?"

"I don't know. All our horses have been stolen, the team horses and the cart horses; Daddy probably went to look for them. We heard that the thieves had gotten as far as the Prussian border with those horses."

"As far as the Prussian border; there's a thing . . . Has 'Daddy' been gone a long time looking for the horses?"

"Quite long."

"How many weeks would that be?"

"I don't remember; four, maybe five."

"He's really making a thorough search for those horses. While for our part we're well aware that Daddy's not so far away. We also know that you're harboring an insurgent in the manor. Who is he? Is it your father?"

"There's no one in the manor besides myself and the old cook, Szczepan Podkurek."

"We shall see. But I advise you to tell us where the rebel is, and show us his hiding place voluntarily. I'm an old man, and I don't like punishing someone without good cause; but if I find the wounded man, it won't be pleasant for him or for you. I won't be so forbearing anymore. Well then?"

"There's no wounded man here. Take a look."

"There's no need to invite me; I'm the one giving the orders here. My information is reliable and exact. A few days ago a wounded man entered the courtyard; the whole village saw him, and he never left. Where is he?"

"Maybe he did come into the courtyard; lots of people walk through here. The fences have all been broken up, and the buildings burned down. How can anyone know anything for sure?"

"So you won't show me where his hiding place is?"

"I won't show you because I don't know of any. There's no one in this house."

The major nodded to an NCO standing by the door, and a moment later a detachment of soldiers with lanterns came into the room. Some of them immediately began to look under the sofas, in the cupboards, behind and on top of the stoves, while others entered the neighboring rooms, moving furniture aside, turning things upside down, and tapping on the walls and the floor. Two junior officers ordered Miss Salomea to open the locked door of the great drawing room. She told Szczepan to fetch the key and open the door. The old man went into the next room and took so long searching for the key that their suspicions were aroused and their greed enflamed. When he finally came back with the key, he offered it to one of the officers. The latter yelled at him viciously:

"Open it yourself, you moron!"

The old man didn't even blink. He stood without moving. Holding the key in his outstretched hand, he said: "I'm not going to open that door, and I'm not going in there."

"How dare you! Open it this instant!"

"I will not. Open it yourselves."

"Why won't you open the door for us, my dear fellow?" asked the major affably.

"Because I have no business going in there."

"Why?"

"The room belongs to the masters . . ."

"What do you mean, the masters?"

"It was the late master's, God rest his soul. Go in there if you want, but I'm not going to."

"Why not?"

"Because the late master doesn't like people walking around and creating a disturbance," muttered the cook.

"What nonsense are you spouting, you old fool?"

"It's the truth."

"What is this? Why won't he go into the room?" asked the major, turning to Miss Brynicka.

"He's telling you the truth," she murmured reluctantly.

"What do you mean?"

"Mr. Rudecki's brother, Dominik, died long ago, but he still occupies those rooms."

The officers laughed derisively. The major asked: "And I daresay you've seen this dead man occupying the rooms?"

"I've not seen him, but I've heard him shifting things about in there, walking around, banging, moving the barrels from one place to another."

The officers exchanged glances, in agreement that it was here the fugitive was concealed. One of them pushed Szczepan forward to light the way with a lantern. But the old cook resisted and stepped back, saying:

"Your Honors can go in on your own."

"Silence! Lead the way!"

"You've come and you'll go away again, but I have to stay here with him . . ."

"With who, you idiot?"

"With the master, with Mr. Dominik."

"So you knew him?"

"Of course I knew him; I worked for him."

"But he's dead now!"

"I'm not so stupid as to go against his wishes."

They turned the key in the lock and opened the door to the great drawing room. It swung back stiffly, with a creak; there was a cracking of the varnish on the floor, which had stuck permanently to the lower boards of the door. The room had the cold and damp smell of emptiness. When lanterns were brought in for illumination, the officers beheld vats hooped with metal bands, casks made of massive staves, barrels, and kegs, all standing in rows. Between them hung old spiders' webs covered with a thick layer of dust. The waxed floor shone. Gilded moldings in the stucco gleamed on the walls, and a fading plafond loomed in the center of the ceiling. On one wall there hung a portrait of a man with stern, handsome features and a malevolent smile. Aside from the picture, nothing was left of the furniture and decorations of the former drawing room. The rows of vats that stood there conveyed a sense of savagery and madness to those looking on.

The officers walked up to the vats and peered into each one, holding their lanterns over them to see whether the insurgent might not be hiding at the bottom. But a thorough search convinced them that all the containers were empty. Then they opened one more door, the one that led from the drawing room into the room where Dominik Rudecki had lived and subsequently had taken his own life. Here the newcomers' eyes encountered an even more unpleasant sight. It was a long, empty room with the blinds pulled down. Here and there were a few wickerwork chairs. Crumpled sheets of paper lay scattered about the floor. Szczepan, who had been forced into the two rooms and pushed ahead to light the way, was all atremble, crossing himself and casting his eyes about into the corners. The officers inspected the floor, walls, windows, and door and determined that there was no other exit; they then turned to leave.

The rooms had made a disagreeable impression on all of them. Everyone had gooseflesh. It wasn't that they were afraid of anything, but they felt a curious, horrible unease. It really did seem as if in these two rooms, which for years had been completely locked up, someone had been standing before the visitors to the house and greeting them with a terrifyingly sardonic superciliousness. Slowly, so as not to betray their unease, the officers left the great drawing room; the lanterns were brought out and the door locked once again. It was only now everyone felt that "the other side" was in reality a loathsome place and understood that it was impossible to dwell there.

With redoubled diligence they set about searching the rooms that were still used, though at present completely unoccupied. They rummaged through everything and turned everything upside down yet found nothing suspicious. They paid particular attention to Miss Salomea's room. It contained little in the way of furniture, so the soldiers put all the more energy into stripping the bed and poking about in the small couch. In the absence of anything whatsoever of interest, they were about to shift their attentions to the kitchen, the larder, and the adjoining closets, when one of the men noticed traces of blood on the underside of the mattress. He informed the commanding officer and his subordinates, who came down to the bedroom and examined the mattress closely.

Miss Brynicka stood by her bedding, surrounded by the officers, who stared at her, brutal, relentless, and mocking. In response to the major's question as to what this blood on the mattress signified, she remained silent. Her face was pale, her eyes cast down. In her compressed lips, in her broad, majestic eyebrows, and in her lowered eyelids there was such scornful pride and such indifference that the officers were driven to reprisal.

"What is the meaning of these bloodstains?" insisted the major.

She said nothing.

"Where did the blood on this mattress come from?"

She said nothing.

"Tell me what this means."

She said nothing.

"What is this?" shouted one of the officers, thrusting the bloody mattress in her face.

"It's a bloodstain," she replied evenly.

"And whose blood is it?"

"Mine."

As she uttered this word, heroic and self-denying, laying down the highest sacrifice of her maidenhead before all these armed men, she suddenly began to burn with all the blood that coursed in her veins. She felt as if her blood would drown her and her shame choke her. The officers murmured and snickered, nudging each other and making humorous asides. Miss Salomea recovered her calm. She listened with composure to their snide comments, whispered jokes, and sarcastic coughs. At one point she raised her eyes and took them all in in a single glance of boundless contempt. In that glance there gleamed the notion, known only to her and contained within her silence, that among all these men she alone, a ridiculed woman, was the only true officer. The old major, father of a large family with grown daughters and a longtime resident of Poland, scratched his sideburns and said something to his subordinates. To the officer in charge of the search he said:

"Go on, check the other rooms! Look sharp now! There's nothing of interest here."

He himself went out into the adjoining room. Here the officers were drinking from canteens, some sitting on the couch, others on the sofa, and the rest simply lying stretched out on the floor in their uniforms.

The search continued through the other wing of the manor, in the kitchen and pantry and in the storehouses and woodsheds. An NCO came in and reported that nothing suspicious had been found around the manor. In the pantry there wasn't so much as a crumb of bread or an ounce of flour. The officers cursed and groaned.

Miss Salomea remained in her room alone, deep in thought. Beside her on the table stood a lantern, illuminating her face and figure. The officers in the drawing room gazed at her and were unable to tear their eyes away. One thin, bony blond fellow with a drooping mustache who was lying on the carpet nudged his comrade with his foot and whispered with a sigh:

"Quite a girl!"

"A real beauty," agreed the other.

"A painted lady," put in a third uninvited.

A moment later they began whispering again:

"What a lass!"

The major, grunting on the broadest sofa, muttered to the admirers:

"Come on, gentlemen, that's enough. You should be sleeping instead of whispering to each other."

"It's hard to get to sleep . . ."

"Just close your eyes and drop off . . ."

"It's hard even to close your eyes."

"Nothing will come of it, you know."

"These are just platonic sighs."

"Platonic sighing is fine so long as it's done quietly, with everyone in his bed. Now, I'd like to get a few minutes' shut-eye, at least."

A dragoon officer by the name of Vesnitsyn, tall and straight as a poplar, came in from outside to report that he had ordered a thorough search of the barn, where one of the partitions was filled with hay, and that all the horses from his unit had been taken in there. He further informed the major that his whole platoon had settled down for the night on the hay, that sentries had been posted at intervals, and that everything was in order. The major thanked the cavalry officer for his report and for carrying out his orders to the letter; then he turned over and settled down to sleep. Miss Salomea heard the report and thought about what it signified. Her heart palpitated and almost stopped.

Vesnitsyn, the tall dragoon officer, sat on an empty chair in a dark corner of the drawing room. He stared through the lighted door of the room at the young woman standing beyond it. He experienced happiness and torment at once. During the long rains, on cold marches through woods and along outlandish trails, he had dreamed of the moment when he would see this creature. Her face and her figure dwelled within him, like a magical apparition, the falsehood of dreams, desire and oblivion, rapture, passion, longing . . .

He had seen this beauty once before, when he had found himself in the region on one of the first days after the outbreak of the uprising. He remembered her from the first glance; he was captivated once and for all. Something sounded in him, like some mysterious, extraordinary music, at the memory of that face. He yearned for it day and night. How terribly he wished that his orders would take him to those parts, that at least once again in his life he would enter that manor! To see her, to look upon her! Only to look . . . ! And destiny had given him this moment. Fortune had not only enabled him to come here, but had also opened the door. She stood there all alone, abandoned by the whole world. A tempest raged in the officer's soul as he leaned on his hand and watched.

A soldier armed with a rifle stood at the door leading to the hallway. Miss Salomea was unable to go into the kitchen to confer with Szczepan. She sat on the bed, and resting her head on her hands, she waited. Her heart reverberated in her breast like a bell. It seemed to her that the sleeping men would hear its beating and that this alarm would give everything away. Every murmur, every rustle, presaged disaster. How endless were the minutes of that night!

In the meantime, Szczepan had been dragged around to show the outbuildings, the cellar in the garden, the ruins of the distillery, and the holes left from the potato clamps; after the whole area had been inspected, he stood by as the soldiers prepared to spend the night in the barn. He watched them lead in the horses and dig out whole armfuls of hay for the animals. He listened intently with his deaf ears . . . The soldiers clambered on top of the piled hay, and after spreading out their greatcoats, they dropped down and slept, both in the corners and right over the insurgent's hiding place.

He wondered if he was still alive, or if he was on his last legs. In his simpleminded sincerity and his sense of powerlessness, he asked God for the latter. He ought to be standing by the young lady, who was alone with the officers, but he couldn't leave, because the dragoon sergeant major wouldn't let him out of his sight. Szczepan thought about what to do if they set fire to the barn and if there wasn't some way of saving the "beanpole" concealed there.

The fat, bearded sergeant major ordered him to bring some hay and make a mattress on the earthen floor of the barn. The old cook worked away, listening as best as his deafness would allow. He danced around the sergeant major, doing everything he was told to, nodding and agreeing to everything and grinning at him, baring the gap in his upper teeth. The sergeant major drove him hither and thither, pushing him about mercilessly and yawning at the top of his voice. So the old man scurried to and fro, bringing more hay, spreading it out evenly, and building a kind of pillow at one end, all the while ingratiating himself slavishly with the sergeant major.

When the latter finally collapsed on the pallet that had been prepared for him, still in his greatcoat and boots, Szczepan hunkered down in the corner, curled up into a ball, and, trying not to draw attention to himself, stared into the impenetrable darkness and waited. They forgot about him. From every side came the sound of the soldiers' snoring. The horses snorted.

The old man began slowly and cautiously crawling up the mound of hay toward where the hiding place was. He did this adroitly, skirting round the soldiers as they slept. When he found the place, no one was lying directly over it, so he dug down into the hay and laid his ear to the board, listening with all his might. Not a sound, not a whisper, reached him from below. Nothing. The clop of horses' hooves on the barn floor, the rustle of hay, the jangling of iron stirrups and snaffles, the sleepy mutterings of the soldiers . . . and finally the eternal inner murmur of his old man's deafness, like the echo of a boundless ocean that absorbs everything into itself. He gave a sigh. He felt sorry for the young man who had been carried here with such difficulty only to die in this place. He regretted his own work, which had seemed such a good idea.

"May he rest in peace . . ." He sighed, staring toward the black vacuum he had dug out with his own hands, and which he could virtually see beneath him. Within him a struggle was going on, and he felt a persistent, powerful urge to move aside the lid and haul the wretched fellow out; but his peasant common sense prevented him. Szczepan lay for a long time in that spot, in a dull, helpless agony that was crueler than words could tell. His old heart was bleeding, long after its tears had all been shed.

Still on all fours, he crawled to a hole in the roof that only he knew, slipped outside, and climbed down a ladder to the ground. He passed shadowlike across the garden, behind the barn, and through the weeds and the broken fences; in the dark he sneaked past the sentries and, like a noiseless specter, entered the kitchen. He felt his way across the kitchen and the adjoining hallway. A stream of light shone through the keyhole into the dark passage. Szczepan placed his eye to the opening and saw Miss Mija sitting on the bed, her head propped up on her hands. Something like the joyful barking of a dog on a dark night resounded in his old, deaf being, in that dark region of the spirit where there was only solitude and loathing. And he remained there, behind the soldier's back, behind the door, his eye to the keyhole, hunched and sleepless on the threshold.

IV

Early in the morning the soldiers assembled, fell into line, and moved out. A thick sleet was falling; the wind howled. The men were hungry, tired, short on sleep, and in ill humor even before they began their march. Last to leave the property at Niezdoły was the cavalry platoon that had occupied the barn. The visitors left behind piles of trash and filth and a foul smell both in the house and in the courtyard.

Miss Salomea stood on the veranda and watched the ranks of soldiers disappearing into the gray morning. She trembled with an inner chill. She longed to run as fast as she could to the barn and lift the wounded man out of his hiding place. But instead of going to the barn, Szczepan climbed the stairs that led from the kitchen to the attic. She hurried after him. The old man crept up to the little skylight and watched the soldiers as they vanished into the mist. When she pleaded with him to set aside these precautions, he responded with a scornful silence.

Squeezing herself into the alcove beneath the skylight, she started to watch, too, curious what the old man could see so far away that was so important. She noticed nothing unusual. Dark, square blocks of infantry were moving along the road between the meadows; they entered a distant village by the woods and finally vanished from sight. They were followed at a distance of a third of a mile by the ruddy-colored detachment of dragoons. The horses and riders merged into a solid mass of singular shape that seemed to be tearing the gray day asunder.

Her eyes dulled from lack of sleep, Miss Salomea was staring at this dark shape when the cook suddenly nudged her and gave a contemptuous laugh. He was peering out and pointing at something.

She looked too and saw that a fragment of the mass of dragoons had broken off from its corner and was rapidly covering the ground in the opposite direction.

"What's going on?" she asked.

"They're trying to fool us and catch us red-handed. Come on, let's go downstairs, and each of us to his own station."

"You think they're coming back here?"

"Of course!"

"But they searched everywhere . . ."

"I know their ways. Come on!"

They hastened downstairs. Szczepan went into the kitchen, lit a fire, and calmly set about scrubbing the pots and pans. There came the noises of his labors, regular, unchanged for decades; and also the sound of a monotonous, grating little song that he always sang under his breath, a clumsy, distorted version of a tune heard from the masters:

"My mother's soup, God rest her soul,
Had beetles floating in the bowl . . ."

Miss Salomea took up some handiwork and sat in waiting in the window of the large room where the officers had slept. She had been there less than a quarter of an hour when she heard the sound of galloping hooves and of horses being pulled up short. The dragoon officer Vesnitsyn flung open the door, ran across the hall, and stood on the threshold of the room. His flashing eyes took in the lone inhabitant of the manor.

She stood up when he came in and looked at him, waiting disdainfully. He did not take off his cap or untie his hood. Water dripped from his boots and from the leather straps of his accoutrements. A few enlisted men came into the room with him. With a nod he instructed them to search the manor. The soldiers moved off into the various rooms of the house. Vesnitsyn was left alone with the young woman. He looked at her in his unflagging, mad enchantment. He murmured in Polish with a Russian accent:

"I doubt you expected such guests . . ."

She shrugged and said nothing. This disconcerted and disarmed him. He did not know what to say. He waited for the results of the new search. After a while he muttered awkwardly and superfluously by way of an explanation:

"I'm not here of my own will . . . I was given an order. And orders are orders . . ."

She paid no attention to what he said. Aware from the officer's looks and movements of the impression her beauty made upon him, she consciously and deliberately made herself a hundred times more beautiful, and from the whole power of her assured charm she created a defensive shield for herself. She sat in the corner of the couch and began sewing indifferently, humming under her breath, as if no one else were in the room with her. She yawned nonchalantly. She rubbed her cold hands together. She looked out the window. The officer stood where he was, staring at her through eyes that were covered by a film of rapture and longing. After a while, seeing that the soldiers conducting the search had not yet returned, she asked superciliously:

"Am I under arrest here?"

"No."

"I'm cold. I want to take a shawl from my bedroom."

"By all means."

"You can send a soldier with me to watch me taking my shawl."

"There's no need."

"How very gracious!"

She went into her room and, sitting at the window, stared out at the world. Through the open door the officer continued to look askance at her. The soft light of the gloomy day fell upon her smooth black hair, shimmering like satin; upon the immaculate form of her neck; upon the pink of her cheeks; upon her long arched eyebrows and her crimson lips. The image her figure created turned his enchantment to madness. Every movement of her head was the form and motion of perfection. When she sighed, the officer's heart was struck by unspeakable remorse. And her scornful gaze brought the blow home like a missile bringing down shame upon him. The world in which her thoughts wandered and through which her soul passed, the realm where her sorrow dwelled, was a stunning vision of beauty that closed up the moment it was glimpsed.

The officer did not move from where he stood. When the soldiers returned and reported that they had not found anything suspicious, he turned about and, without another word or another glance, left, jumped into the saddle, and rode away at the head of his unit.

Miss Salomea did not turn round, either. She was crying. Bitter tears streamed from her eyes as she felt the constant hardship in which she lived. She imagined that the insurgent hidden in the hay had suffocated or had bled to death. She thought of her father, wasting away in army bivouacs; about her cousins who had perished so terribly and at such an early age; of all those who had gone from this house. She reminded herself of the unease and the nighttime terror that lay in wait after the present day and would go on for untold numbers of endless nights . . . She contemplated the brutal power that nothing could break, whose cruelty nothing could stem.

What would she do if Szczepan ran away? What would she do if they hanged him after they found the insurgent? What would she do if none of her relatives returned to this accursed house, where Dominik alone reigned in triumph? She was racked with a dull, blind pain. Despair shook her as a gale shakes the branches of trees. She no longer wanted to think about anything, to take on any of the jobs that needed to be done. For so many nights now she had been without sleep, exhausted, chilled within, and on edge. She wept without relief and without any hope of consolation, leaning over the side of the bed.

The door handle creaked. The old man came in. He scowled at the woman and muttered something, as was his wont. He shrugged.

"We should go. What's all this blubbering?"

"Go where?"

"To get him. You can't be sure—"

"Come on, then!"

"But first we should look to check."

"They won't come back a third time."

"Who knows, the bastards may have left a spy to keep an eye on things."

"We'll watch out."

"Listen, Miss Bawlomea, instead of wailing to no purpose, why don't you go outside and take a stroll about the garden. Have a look to see if there isn't anyone there. One of them may even be watching from up on the hill."

"I'll go up the hill!"

"Good idea. Just act casual, as if you was out for a stroll. Stop and have a peek around, then move on. From the hill you'll have a good view of the whole area. And if you see anyone hanging about, let me know at once."

"All right, I'm off."

She slipped outside and went for a walk just as Szczepan had told her. She slowly climbed the hill, overgrown with juniper and brush, that rose up immediately beyond the garden. Snow made wet by the rain lay on the ground. It nestled in hollows and under bushes. How horrible that place was when seen from above! Burned buildings, broken fences, the garden chopped down and half-blackened with fire . . . A wasteland . . . The old manor dark and deserted, as if it were stricken by disgrace . . . This was Niezdoły, where the whole neighborhood had made merry for so many years, where the revels had gone on till morning, then through the rest of the day after the ball, and into the night again, till they dropped . . .

Miss Mija noticed no one as she looked around. Not a soul was moving in the surroundings. The soldiers had long ago disappeared into the woods. She hid among the bushes and stared out watchfully. At last! . . . Szczepan came out of the kitchen and went down in the direction of the river. He loitered outside the garden, wandered behind the distillery, and kept turning back. Finally, once he had inspected everything thoroughly, he quickly entered the barn. Long minutes passed. Miss Salomea's heart began to pound in her breast. It seemed to her that whole hours had gone by since the old man had opened the barn door. She couldn't wait. She hurried stealthily down the hill, crossed the garden and the courtyard, stole into the barn, and clambered up onto the hay.

Contrary to her expectations, Szczepan did not greet her with abuse. He had removed the lid from over the hole and was trying to pull out the injured man. He was having difficulties. Whenever he got him halfway up the shaft, he would lose his footing on the hay and fall on his back, and Odrowąż would slide back down into his grave. The wounded man was groaning in his dark dungeon. The other two were delighted when they heard his moans and redoubled their efforts. Szczepan instructed Miss Salomea to wrap the end of one of the ropes around her shoulder and pull. He took the other rope and hooked it likewise around his shoulder. They each set about pulling in different directions, tugging at the cords with all their might. In this way they hauled the poor insurgent to the surface.

Once he was out, they ascertained that he was still alive, though weakened and half-suffocated. Szczepan ordered Miss Salomea to go up the hill again and scan the area. From the other end of the barn he fetched a wheelbarrow that was used for transporting firewood. He lifted the sick man, laid him in the wheelbarrow, covered him with hay, on top of that piled some dry kindling from the corner of the barn, and wheeled it all into the kitchen. There he removed the fur coat and the boots from the sick man, cleaned him off, and brushed him down, then carried him into the bedroom and laid him in the bed.

When Miss Salomea returned home, she found her patient already in a made-up bed. He was only half-conscious and excessively red and swollen. His eyes were bloodshot and staring, his face livid. His wounds had opened and had soaked through his bandages to such an extent that they had to put down thick sackcloth sheets over the bedclothes so they would not once again have bloody stains as testimony against them. Miss Salomea set about changing the bandages and redressing the wounds.

Some of the bandages had slipped down, leaving the wounds exposed. As she dressed them anew, she experienced a curious sensation she had never known before. She began to sense each wound in her own being—and not just to see it, but to feel it, too, so that her own body suffered in the same places as the wounded man's. On her head, beneath her eye, on her arms, between her ribs, and on her right hip there appeared as it were stigmata, copies, living images of the real wounds. As she attended to the cuts and injuries, the blows and bruises, she began to know them, to understand them, and to grasp the entirety of their bizarre, sublime life. Without disgust she looked upon the seeping blood and the living, lacerated body. When she finished the dressings the winter's evening was already drawing on. The sick man fell asleep in a profound fever.

She collapsed on the couch and fell sound asleep herself. How happy she was when she awoke to see a radiant day! That meant the night had passed without searches or ghosts; she had managed to sleep through it unbroken from beginning to end. Her canary, her only friend, had burst out singing in the window at the sight of such glorious sunshine. For some unknown reason, the canary bore the mysterious name of Pupinetti. He had a black cap or crown of dark feathers, though for the rest he was pure yellow. Miss Mija greeted him affectionately with an exclamation that had somehow long ago found its way into their relations:

"A bas la calotte!"

Pupinetti inclined his head and, puffing out his throat, began to sing a song of praise to the sun that was the merriest, most joyful tune under that sun. Seeing that his mistress was coming up to him, he began to hop from bar to bar and to rock on his swing. He pecked at a grain of kasha and scratched a scrap of cabbage leaf. He took a drink of water and called his friend with a rapid, delighted cry. He was not afraid of her threatening call—*A bas la calotte!*—or of her hand as it entered his cage. He only cocked his head, as if he were in fact a little worried for his cap, as she took him in her hand and kissed him on the bill with the most gorgeous lips on earth.

The sick man opened his eyes, half-blinded by the fever. He turned his reddened face toward his nurse. His swollen lips uttered some incomprehensible sound. Miss Salomea stood over him with Pupinetti in her hand and showed the poor warrior the bird. As he noticed the canary, he recognized what it was. He gave a pathetic smile. Miss Salomea released the bird from her hand. Trained to perch on her pillow, Pupinetti flew to the head of the unknown intruder's bed, sat on the headboard, and shook and straightened his feathers. He sang the blithest and most radiant of his songs. The wounded man smiled again. He forgot about the torments of life and listened, enraptured.

V

The next few nights passed without incident. There were no intruders in the great deserted manor. The injured insurgent spent whole days and nights in a febrile sleep. They couldn't tell whether the fever was caused by his wounds or by some other internal sickness. The swelling round his eye went down considerably, and the black bruising began to clear up. His eyelid appeared, and beneath it a healthy pupil that was able to see. At this point the laceration under the eye was dressed with lint and the cheek was bandaged once again.

As the marks of cuts and blows began to disappear, it was as if a different face began to emerge from underneath the swollen wounds. The sharp, well-formed nose took on a new shape, and a pale, intelligent forehead could be seen over dark eyebrows. The head wounds were the fastest to heal. The hair, which had long gone uncut and which from time to time Miss Salomea washed and combed, seemed by itself to act like the lint in healing the scars, which were still red but were now dry.

Worst of all was the bullet wound in the man's hip. He was unable to make the simplest movement without experiencing a fearful agony. It was clear that the bullet had worked its way down among the sinews and veins, because the pain came from ever lower points in his thigh. The wound was still open and was festering revoltingly. Constant washing and cleaning did no good.

One night the nurse was woken by a knocking at the windows and doors, though of a different kind from that made by Ryfka. Someone was banging over and over again, insistently. There was also a hammering at the windows of the uninhabited part of the building and at the door to the garden. Szczepan, who had been awakened at once, had no time to carry the wounded man outside, since the whole property obviously was surrounded. Instead, in the dark he and Miss Salomea together carried the poor fellow in his bedclothes as fast as they could to Dominik's drawing room, where they placed him in one of the empty vats. They barely had time to do this when the hammering rose to a crescendo. The moment the door was opened it turned out that, fortunately, these were Poles.

It was the remains of a regiment that had become separated from Kurowski's army after the terrible defeat at Miechów;* they had been on forced marches, evading the Russian columns under Chernitski and Ostrovski, wandering about forests, backwoods, and ravines, pursued day and night, till in the darkness they had happened upon Niezdoły. After two commanders had fled, one after the other, the unit had no commanding officer. It was made up of men who were starving, freezing cold, thoroughly exhausted, and utterly broken in spirit. They were no longer fusiliers; they were not armed with scythes, or even with staves, as was so common in the uprising; they were virtually defenseless.

They had scarcely come in when they dropped down side by side on the floor and began snoring as a man. Some of them went off to search the manor for food and vodka. They looked in the pantry, the kitchen, and the other rooms, but they found nothing. Miss Salomea was forced to accompany them in their search. When they had opened every jar and every chest and had turned up nothing at all, in their hunger and their desperation they began to make threats. One of them pulled a pistol from his belt and, with a savagery close to madness, placed the muzzle against the young woman's forehead.

She met his hellish gaze with indifference and waited for the shot. The wretched brute did not remove the pistol; he also did not know what to do next. He stood with his weapon pointed between Miss Salomea's beautiful eyes and turned paler and paler.

*The battle of Miechów took place on February 17, 1863.—TRANS.

"Why don't you pull the trigger?" she asked.

"Don't ask me again!"

"So either shoot or continue your search; bluffing is a waste of time."

"Where's the kasha?"

"There's a little kasha, but it's very much needed for those who live here, and for one wounded man."

"Where is it?"

"We'll take a look right away. First put down your pistol; it ought to be aimed at the enemy, not between the eyes of defenseless women in pantries."

"Be quiet! Where's the kasha?"

Szczepan, who was standing just behind Miss Salomea, put a word in.

"There's not very much of that kasha; not enough to feed all of you. I'll fetch some potatoes."

"Where are they?"

"There's still a handful in one of the clamps."

"How much?"

"Like I say, there'll be a quarter of a bushel; perhaps half a bushel can be scraped together."

"Will they be frozen?"

"Not necessarily; they were properly covered."

"Where are they?"

"They are where they are. I'll bring them myself. If everyone goes, they'll trample on them and squash them. You won't have anything to eat."

"We'll eat as much as we want to!"

"Then what will we give the others when they come by here?"

"They can feed on dirt!"

"They'll put a gun to our heads again."

"Shut the hell up, Granddad!" yelled the starving insurgent.

He seized the old man by the collar and shook him repeatedly. But Szczepan pulled away boldly, twisting his shoulder from the other man's grip. Miss Salomea came to his assistance. She pushed his assailant away forcefully. The latter glared at her with a ferocious look that bode no good. She sensed mindless rage in his eyes. At any moment he might raise the pistol and pull the trigger. In order to calm him, she started to try to turn the whole thing into a joke; and in an attempt to turn his passion in a different direction, she told an anecdote about the cook.

"You can see," she began, "that his front teeth are missing . . ."

"I'll smash in the rest of them for him!"

"Before you knock out the rest of those old teeth, just listen to the story of the ones he's already lost."

"I couldn't care less about his teeth!"

"Well, that's a fine way to converse with a lady!"

"'Converse' . . . Tell your story, then, miss, since it's so important . . ."

"But you're not listening. How can I speak?"

"I am listening; it's just that you can't hear the hunger screaming inside me."

"It's not a long story; your hunger can listen, too. You see, it was like this. When this old man of ours was still a boy, he served the cook in this very same manor as a kitchen boy. Before he knew what was going on, he was called up to the army. He realized he'd miss the kitchen, with all the pans and the sauces; and he was afraid of soldiering—twenty-five years with a gun in your hand is no joke! The village clerk came to take him for his physical. Our kitchen boy hopped round the corner of the manor, took a stone from the ground, and knocked out his two front teeth, which, as you know, with the old flintlock muskets were needed for biting off the charge. The clerk grabbed him by the scruff of the neck and was about to tie him up, when the lad laughed aloud and showed the bloody gap at the front of his mouth."

"What of it?"

"Nothing; the moral of the story is simply that there's no point in pushing people around for any old reason! And he got up to many more tricks of that kind."

"I'll take the liberty of postponing any other little stories till later, when we've peeled the potatoes. *Primum edere, deinde philosophari.* Do you know what that means, miss?"

"I don't, though it must be something to do with food."

"Exactly . . . Come on, then! Where's that sack?"

He found the sack, went off with Szczepan, and came back shortly afterward with the potatoes.

They lit a fire with wood chopped from the pickets of the broken fence. Everyone set to work peeling the potatoes. It transpired that the soldiers had among their riches a hunk of lard taken from somewhere. Szczepan went out into the night and brought back in the bottom of the sack a peck or so of kasha from his hiding place. He set about cooking the potatoes and the kasha with great culinary expertise. But he also ran out time and again to stand sentry—to listen with his deaf ears in case the ground was groaning under the feet of the enemy infantry on their way to the manor . . .

VI

Not only did the injury in the insurgent's hip not heal, it began to be dangerous. Below the entry wound, in the groin, there began to form a large abscess that caused the sick man so much pain, he shouted for hours on end; not even the thought of the safety of the house and concern for his own life could silence his inhuman cries, which sounded like an animal's howling. Miss Salomea did not sleep at all at night; she didn't even lay her head on her pillow, for fear of an unexpected intrusion by the soldiers.

It became pointless to carry the duke to the barn after the Jewish girl had given her warning knock on the window—he would moan from his place of concealment in the hay. Once, hearing noises in the barn, an officer had instructed his unit to walk up and down across the whole partition, thrusting their bayonets deep into the hay. It was only by exceptional good fortune that they did not hit upon the hiding place; and it was only because the hay-filled barn was a good place to spend the night that the officer refrained from ordering it to be burned.

It was obvious that the bullet was dropping toward the knee, inflicting untold agony and causing the formation of abscesses. In such circumstances life was unutterably hard. Miss Salomea decided that there was nothing for it but to summon a surgeon. Yet she had no idea how to do this, since she didn't have a penny—everything she owned had been taken away by the soldiers who had passed through in the course of the winter—and she did not have use of a horse or sleigh. It wasn't safe to hire a cart in the village, as the farmers were hostile and the presence of the sick man at the manor might get out. Yet she didn't have the heart to throw him out of the house.

He himself had hit upon a sure solution. One day, as she was standing by the bed, feeding him, he suddenly reached into the pocket of her dress and pulled out the pistol she had shown him when he first arrived. She took the pistol from his hands. But from then on, hour after hour, howling in agony, he entreated her to end his miserable existence with a shot between the eyes. Whenever he could reach her arms, he would seize them with feverish hands like white-hot iron pincers and implore her to end his life. How many pleas, and what arguments to accompany them, he uttered as he begged for that single shot!

So many had perished! Good, noble, courageous men . . . Russian boots had trampled them into the mud of the open field! They had died of their wounds, without succor, in the woods, without glory—for nothing! The holy ideal had tumbled from its altar! After the defeat at Miechów, Polish farmers had put the wounded into wagons, taken them to the authorities, and handed them over to their executioners. The steadfast servility of the mighty and the fearful ignorance of the poor had gone hand in hand . . . What foolishness, what tyranny amid so many dangers it was to prolong his powerless suffering! He wanted to die! Not to know what was going on and what had happened to him! Not to remember! Not to have to endure the hell of humiliation as he had to be concealed in the hay from the Russian soldiers!

"Woman!" he would exclaim. "Have mercy! Kill me! Let me kill myself! I don't want to live! You can bury me easily at night down by the river, at the place where I washed the blood from my wounds. You can return in the spring and plant a flower there. I'll be happy . . ."

In despair, and with no idea what to do, without even telling Szczepan, Miss Salomea went one evening to see her friend Ryfka. The lights were already out at the inn, and the doors were locked tight. Out of fear of intrusion, the windows had been boarded up on the outside with lengths of planking so that inside the only daylight came from the cracks in between the boards. Miss Mija began fiddling with one of the windows, loosening the nails holding the planks tightly in place, and picking at the clay that was put there to keep in the warmth; and eventually she got it open. Then, slipping through the opening a long piece of fencepost she had brought with her, she set about poking it blindly toward where she knew from experience Ryfka was asleep on the couch.

For a long time she was unsuccessful, as the little Jewish girl was sound asleep, having been so often woken at night. Finally, realizing at once who was summoning her, she jumped up to the window. She whispered through the crack in the boards, so quietly that it sounded like the soughing of the wind, so as not to wake the other members of her family, who were asleep in the same room and those adjoining.

Miss Salomea explained briefly what the problem was. Horses were needed. She must have horses and a sleigh for one night. She had to drive to the town as fast as possible, come back, and then return there once again; and not a soul could know about it. Ryfka should borrow the horses from someone. And since hiring a cart cost money, which she didn't have, she'd probably have to take it without asking. It would be given back later.

How could it be done? Ryfka took fright. How could it be done? Oy, oy! A pair of horses and a sleigh, two trips to town and back in a single night . . . Oy, oy! How could it be done? She scratched her tousled head and smacked her lips distractedly. Her voice trembled from cold and from fear, and her teeth chattered loudly.

"Tell me what I should do!" said Miss Mija.

"What can I say? I don't know myself."

"I came all this way just to hear you say that?"

"I'm willing to help, but what can we do?"

"Why are you shaking like that? Are you afraid?"

"Yes."

"Of what?"

"Well, there are some horses here . . . three of them . . . team horses."

"Whose are they?"

"I don't know."

"Where are they from?"

"They were brought in yesterday."

"Stolen?"

"I don't know."

"You don't know! I'm asking you, you silly girl, whether they're stolen!"

"What do you think? That they're a gift from someone?"

"Where are they?"

"In the stables."

"Are they being kept here for someone?"

"How am I supposed to know? It's better for me not to say anything. The horses are in the stables."

"Tell me the truth! It wasn't you who stole them and it's not you who's holding them. So you won't even tell me the truth? Is that what you're really like, you unfaithful Jew!"

"Why would I not tell the truth? They're probably being looked after for someone. Why bother talking about it? There's a guy sleeping in the attic who brought them here."

"When's he traveling on?"

"Tomorrow, at night."

"Which way is he headed?"

"I don't know."

"Give me two of those horses!"

"Oy, oy! I'm scared."

"Be scared, then! They'll be back by morning!"

"I can't! They'll kill me!"

"Who?"

"My father and the man who brought the horses."

"They won't know."

"What do you mean, they won't know! You expect them not to find out about something like that! Who could pull it off?"

"I can! Do you have a sleigh?"

"There's one here, but it's just a little one that belongs to some of the tenants."

"Let it be the tenants'. Come on! Fetch the keys and climb out the hole here!"

Ryfka gave a quiet, desperate sob. She stood on the other side of the window, crying.

"You won't do it?"

"They'll murder me. They'll knock my block off!"

"You'll live."

This argument she somehow found convincing. She calmed down and asked some questions.

"Who would go?"

"I'll go alone."

"And no one will know?"

"No one! Just you and me."

"If they see, if they find out who did it, I'll get a terrible beating, I really will!"

"You poor, delicate little thing!"

"That man who brought the horses . . . he's got this big whip! . . ."

"Fetch the keys!"

Ryfka vanished as silently as a ghost into the depths of the house and for a long time did not reappear again.

Miss Salomea was beginning to think that she would never come back at all. It was still freezing, and there was a biting wind. Moaning gusts eddied about the walls and corners of the dark, silent inn. The night was black and starless. At last the back door, leading onto the rubbish heap that was the courtyard, creaked quietly, and little Ryfka came out of the house. She closed the door gingerly and listened to see if anyone had followed her. Assuring herself that no one had heard her and no one had noticed when she opened the door, she hastened over to the brick-built stables and set to work with great vigor. She hurriedly opened the stable door and then the door of the coach house.

Miss Salomea stepped into the stables and approached the horses confidently. They were snorting uneasily and stamping their hooves in the darkness. She felt their heads and discovered that they were wearing full, high-quality horse collars, in readiness to set off at a moment's notice if need be. The horses were good-sized and clearly well looked after, as they shifted in place and gave fierce snorts. She felt for the fastenings of the reins, the straps of the bridles, the traces, and the cords; then she bridled two of the horses and led them out of the stable. Ryfka had already pushed out of the coach house a small, bare sleigh that truly was in the Jewish style.

The two of them quickly harnessed the horses to the sleigh. In a short moment they had straightened the reins and found the whip. As Miss Salomea sat in the front seat, Ryfka brought an armful of hay from the coach house and threw it in the back of the sleigh so there would be something to give the horses on the way. Then she locked the stable and the coach house as fast as she could. Like a black bat she flitted back in through the door of the inn and closed it quietly. Miss Salomea flicked the reins cautiously and moved at a walk out of the courtyard and into the fields.

She pulled up in front of the veranda of the manor. She hitched the horses to a post and went into the house. She ordered Szczepan to sleep in the sick man's room, by the door to the drawing room, and to keep his ears open. She herself put on warm clothes, took a fur to cover her feet and a rug for the seat, and ran out. She settled herself in the sleigh, took the reins, and gave each of the horses a firm crack of the whip. They started up and dashed away. She crossed a field to bypass the inn, then came out onto an already smoothed road and cracked the whip over and over again. The horses raced along at full tilt. The sleigh rocked from one pothole to the next, gliding over the thick snow.

There were two routes to the town. The longer one led along the road and then the highway; the shorter was the "woodland way." The latter had always been dangerous because there were wolves. At the present moment, however, it was safer—because there were no people. The woodland road led across open country; then through a clearing, between tall bushes, and along cattle paths between pasturelands; then finally into an unbroken, dense, silent forest. Miss Mija shuddered as she passed the open spaces and entered the deep, soundless woods. She sat herself more firmly on the sheaf of straw, planted her shoes against the footboard, lashed the horses around the legs, and galloped through the trees. The road was quite wide; in the summer it was muddy, but now in the snow it was fine. The horses leaped along it, lifting the sleigh behind them like a feather.

An icy fear chilled her to the bone and overwhelmed her heart. An unfamiliar sound came to her ears: she was being chased! They were after her! She could hear their hoofbeats! Who was that racing after the sleigh? Soldiers wasting away in the barbarous war; servants of some human law; bandits who respected no law whatsoever; or beasts who fought with humans? She knew nothing . . . Against everything that might be, one single law rose up within her—pure sentiment. Unaware of this, she believed blindly in the free power of her young soul and in the strength of the free horses. She hurtled along like the wind.

She was amazed to see that there were no longer any trees lining her route. She had passed through the forest unbelievably quickly. She had no more than a couple of miles to go to the town. She let the horses ease off a little and rode more cautiously, keeping her eyes and ears open. After the woods she had to pass by villages, bridges, and lanes and to turn left and right. Her eyes were accustomed to the darkness, and she knew exactly where she was. She correctly followed every turn and curve that she needed.

From the hill by the brick-built inn known as the Old Ridgepole she saw the lights of the town. Her heart gave an anxious beat. She rode off the even highway into the fields bordering the turnpike and moved rapidly toward the suburbs. She sneaked past the slaughterhouse and the military barracks and rode round the backs of gardens, past various sheds, huts, storehouses, brickyards, and windmills, till she came out into some meadows near the park and, swinging round, twisting and turning, reached a fence that ran along one of the paved town streets. On the other side of the fence the footsteps of townspeople still out at this hour could be heard on the stone sidewalk.

Miss Mija climbed out of the sleigh, unbridled the horses, covered them with the rug, and gave them a handful of hay to eat after the ride. She tied the reins tightly to one of the fenceposts. Then, after straightening her clothes and gathering up her skirts, she went into the town. She walked quickly along unlighted side streets, without encountering anybody, till she reached the broad market square. She ran across the middle of the square and slipped into the gateway of a building that contained the apartment of Dr. Kulewski, an eminent physician known throughout the province. It was not especially late, as the gate had not been locked or the lamp in the stairwell turned off.

Miss Salomea rang the doorbell. The door was opened somewhat irritably by an old, hunchbacked maid. She announced that the doctor was already getting ready for bed. Miss Brynicka slipped her last few coins into the woman's hand and asked to be allowed to see the great doctor. She was admitted. She waited for some time. The dim light provided by a wax candle revealed the beautiful furniture that belonged to the doctor, an old bachelor—sofas and armchairs, fixtures and ornaments, embroidered cushions, sumptuous screens, and lithographs in costly frames.

Finally the door opened and the doctor stood on the threshold, his clean-shaven face visibly expressing dissatisfaction. He measured the visitor with a hard gaze. He was a handsome, strong, well-preserved *viveur* of fifty, an excellent doctor, and the town's greatest gourmet. On a number of occasions he had been summoned to Niezdoły to treat the children and adults of the manor for serious illnesses. Miss Brynicka knew him and once, many years ago, had been one of his patients. The doctor took some time to remember her; struck by her extraordinary beauty, he grew more polite and less arrogant. He came up to her with a bow. Miss Salomea reminded him who she was, and, upon being courteously invited, she sat down in an armchair. The doctor was ever more pliant and eager to be of assistance.

Without any introduction, she came directly to the point. She explained the situation. She asked him to put on his fur coat, take his surgical instruments, and ride back with her. The doctor's face clouded over. He refused firmly and categorically. An insurgent, a ten-mile journey, when it was already past ten o'clock at night—out of the question! He would not go. Regrettably! He was extremely sorry! Yes, this was a truly unfortunate business. He himself was a patriot and felt for the cause as much as anyone, perhaps even more than anyone; but nothing could impel him to go with her! He had responsibilities, many patients in the town, maybe other similar cases, maybe other cases more important than this one, maybe much more important, even. Miss Salomea heard him out patiently. At one moment she seized the doctor's gesticulating hand and pressed it to her lips. Then she slipped to the floor and embraced his knees. He pulled away and stepped back.

"Oh, so it's love!" he laughed. "You're in love with this warrior, young lady?"

"No. I'm only doing my duty."

"Is that so? Then why the begging, and why is there such rapture in your eyes?"

"That's simply how I feel."

"The insurgents provoked a great power to war," he lectured her. "They're young upstarts! Lunatics! Thousands of people have to die; this is wartime, do you understand, miss?"

"I do."

"You see, then! This is wartime, so one person cannot have all of our sympathy."

"I'm sure you're right; but it's my job to save the man who was delivered into my hands. He came from the battle, walking in front of our veranda, and he didn't even know where he was going."

"So that's why he's the only one?"

"Please, Doctor, put your coat on and take your instruments and we'll go; time is short."

"Do you imagine for a minute that I'll go with you?"

"I'm not leaving here without you."

The doctor smiled as he looked into her candid, marvelously beautiful eyes, at her pale forehead peeping out from beneath her fur cap, at her pink lips and snowy cheeks, blushing from the heat in the apartment. He was perplexed.

"You'll be the ruin of me! I can't do it. I'm watched, and I'm probably followed . . . I just can't do it!"

"You have to!"

"Is that right? I have to?"

"You have to!"

"Because you're commanding me to?"

"Not me; the Lord God is commanding you to save a poor soldier. I've done all I can by myself. Now I can't do any more. If I could manage on my own, I wouldn't be here kissing your hands and asking for your help! You're a doctor, and I'm just a simple woman. I came to you because it's a doctor's job to find the bullet in the wound."

"Whoever heard such arguments! And what will be my fee?" he asked, looking her brazenly in the eyes.

"Nothing."

"That's quite an incentive!"

"Let's go, Doctor!"

"I'll go on condition that I will receive a fee, which I'll determine myself . . ."

She looked into his eyes in a bold and somewhat mocking fashion and repeated: "Let's go, time is running out!"

The doctor shrugged and went into his surgery. He bustled about there for some time, opening things, shutting them, and putting them in order; then finally he came into the hallway, wearing a fur coat and felt boots. From the hall door he called to Miss Salomea:

"You are literally abducting me from my home. If they stop us on the way, it'll be the end of me."

"I'm taking you to a sick girl at a Jewish inn. No one can hold it against you that you're riding out to see a patient."

"Oh, for sure! In these circumstances, in these times . . . I know what it looks like nowadays to travel by night to visit a sick person."

They left quietly, slipped through the gateway, crossed the square, and, taking the same hellishly dark back streets as before, reached the horses. Fortunately no one had noticed the "team" or stolen the horses.

Miss Salomea, relieved to see this, bridled the horses, spread the rug on the seat for the doctor, and invited him to sit down.

"Where's your servant?" he asked.

"I'm here," she replied.

"Well, I never! I'm not going!"

"Are we back to that?"

"You can't drive—you don't know how."

"In a moment you'll be eating your words . . ."

She sat in front, and stealthily, at a walk, she drove out across parklands and along alleyways into the suburbs and from there into the fields. Then she took the same road, familiar now. She sped gaily through the forest and across the open country. Dr. Kulewski, an old bachelor and a notorious womanizer, attempted to take advantage of this unusual situation. At first he wanted to sit on the front seat and help with the reins; then he offered to put his arm around his charming driver to keep her warm. But the driver threatened to tip him off the sleigh in the middle of the woods and make wolf fodder of him if he didn't sit down on his rug-covered seat and behave himself. In less than an hour and a half they reached Niezdoły.

Miss Salomea approached the place cautiously, passing the inn and looking intently to see whether there weren't any visitors at the manor. Fortunately it was dark everywhere. The lofty old poplars boomed out dull anthems that her heart and ear had known since early childhood. She knocked on the window. Szczepan opened the door and went to take care of the horses, which were hot, foam flecked, and steaming. He took them to the barn, unbridled them, and led them into the partition with the hay. He latched the barn door and returned to the manor.

The doctor had immediately set about examining the sick man. He dressed the wounds to the eye and the head, then on the man's back and between his ribs, and finally the wretched hip wound. He found an abscess that was just beginning to form and decided it should be lanced. Szczepan went outside to stand sentry; Miss Salomea had to fetch and hold the basin and supply warm water, towels, and lint. The doctor cut the swelling open unmercifully, then took a probe and began to search for the bullet in the depths of the wound. The sick man writhed in agony as he was carved up alive. The operation was conducted by the light from a small tallow candle in a lantern. The doctor tired himself out; tugging and struggling, he sought the bullet with his instruments, but for all his fervor he could not locate it. He tried once, twice, thrice; he tried ten times; all to no avail.

The duke lost consciousness time and again from the pain and screamed under the knife; in the end he set about defending himself, hitting out and slapping the doctor and the young lady. The doctor had to give up. The bedding was covered in blood; the floor, the instruments, and the bowls were all bloody, too. At this point the doctor skillfully dressed the hip wound, bandaged all of the wounds, and announced that he would leave. He declared that they would have to wait. The injured man should remain in bed. Miss Salomea instructed Szczepan to bring the horses round. She was extremely despondent; all her efforts had been for nothing. She jumped into the driver's seat, and once the doctor had taken his place, she galloped off back the same way.

How painful that journey was, and how filled with despair! To make matters worse, the doctor refused to conduct himself properly but instead unceremoniously demanded his fee. Exhausted by having to fend him off, ridden by anger, disgust, and spiritual torment, she left the doctor near the town. He got off far from the turnpike, in the fields, and as a precaution made his way back to his hearth and home on foot. Miss Brynicka bade him farewell and raced back homeward. In the small hours of the morning, while it was still completely dark, she returned to Ryfka the stolen horses and the sleigh.

During her absence Szczepan had washed the sick man, changed the bloodied sheets and clothing, and washed the blood from the floor and the furniture. Odrowąż was moaning in his sleep. Miss Salomea went to bed weary in body and spirit, filled with scorn and with an inner chill.

VII

One night soon after that, after all her toils and tribulations, she had fallen into the deepest of sleeps. The sick insurgent, still half-conscious from the fever, dozed in the darkened room. He was visited by fleeting, nightmarish dreams filled with monstrous visions.

All at once he was wrenched out of his state of semiconsciousness by the sound of a horse's hooves outside. The duke clearly heard someone ride up to the manor on horseback and edge warily along the wall, while the horse shifted from one foot to the other just outside the window. Every thump of a hoof against the ground reverberated in his ear, in his brain, and in his soul. In the gloom, his febrile imagination presented the figure of a dark rider before his eyes. Suddenly there came the soft tapping of a finger against the windowpane, cautious yet insistent. The sick man heard it. He set about waking Miss Mija, calling her more and more loudly. Since she remained sound asleep, he had to get out of bed and hobble on his injured leg to where she slept. He touched her drooping head and tugged at her hair to rouse her. She awoke and for a moment sat on her couch, unable to come to.

He whispered in her ear that someone was knocking at the window. She understood and listened intently. Odrową ż thought it must be something truly terrible, for she began praying quietly, in a painful and timid whisper, through chattering teeth. In a second she jumped up, hurriedly mumbling the last words of the prayer, threw on her warm coat, and with feverishly trembling hands lit the candle in the lantern. She fluttered like a bird into the cold drawing room, opened the front door, and with a stifled cry rushed outside.

The sick man leaned from his bed, watching to see what would happen and whether His Grace would have to be hidden in the barn. From the hallway of the manor he heard joyful exclamations from the young lady, and a moment later, by the light of the lantern, in the drawing room he saw his nurse hugging a tall old man and rocking in his arms. Their embrace was silent, almost ecstatic, and endless. When the newcomer finally released Miss Mija, Odrowąż saw his face. He was a lofty man with gray whiskers wearing a fur-lined jacket, a sheepskin cap, and high-topped boots. The duke surmised that this was Miss Mija's father. Mr. Brynicki, still covered in snow and with icicles dangling from his hair, gazed at his daughter. He whispered something to her, or to himself, as he stroked her head with a hand from which he had not yet removed his rough mitten.

The light from the lantern fell on the bedroom. Glancing into it, the old fellow suddenly saw a man in his daughter's bed and pointed at him in profound astonishment. All in one breath Miss Salomea quickly told the story of the wounded man—his appearance after the battle of Małogoszcz, all their ordeals and accidents, the searches, and her ride into the town.

Old Brynicki listened with a frown, impatient and suspicious. During the story he entered the bedroom. He took off his cap and, holding the lantern high, stared without ceremony at the injured man. The latter raised himself on his elbow and greeted the father of his protectress with a blank smile.

"So where did you get so badly wounded, my friend?" asked the old man.

"At Małogoszcz."

"You got trounced by our honorable compatriot Dobrowolski, along with Golubov and Chengery. You didn't do too well for yourselves there . . ."

"That's true!"

"And your wounds are so bad you even had to take to a young lady's bed to have them dressed?"

"Miss Salomea was kind enough to put me here when I first came."

"So what are these wounds? I'm an old hand, I know a thing or two about wounds. Maybe I'll be able to ease your delicate sufferings."

He lifted the bedsheet brusquely and set about inspecting the wounds on the injured man's head, beneath his eye, on his back, on his chest, and in his hip. Yet this was not a medical examination, but rather an investigation of how things really stood. The old soldier was not moved by the wounds. He muttered advice about applying something or other and recommended that they should keep looking for the bullet by cutting open the area round the wound; the injured man could even do this himself. He said in conclusion:

"If they find you here, friend, they won't just raze everything that's left; you yourself won't be spared, either. It might be better if you hopped over to the woods for your treatment. Spruce branches draw a fever. If you sleep on mud, it'll help to heal those shot wounds of yours. The bullet'd pass out faster, too, because it'd be drawn down to the earth."

"That's what I want, too. If only I were able to stay on my feet and walk!"

Brynicki sat down to rest on the couch and stared at the guest through bloodshot eyes. Miss Salomea crouched at his feet and kissed his hands, his legs, even his leather straps and his threadbare jacket bespattered with snow and mud.

"These boots of mine are all torn up! The damn things let in water! Tell Szczepan to look for my other pair. They're worn, too, but they'll be better than these. Though make sure he greases them thoroughly with tallow!"

"Tallow," she whispered regretfully.

"Isn't there any?"

"Not a drop."

"Never mind; I'll just have to put them on as they are. How many weeks have I had these same footcloths on! Go and look for some shirts for me, darling. I'll take whatever there is. I'll get changed, then I'm off!"

"Again!?"

"What is it, my little sparrow?"

"Oh, my goodness!"

"Things are bad for us, sparrow . . . These are bad times. And there'll be worse to come . . . We'll make it through! There've been times even worse than this before. In Siberia, darling . . . This is nothing! Keep smiling!"

"I've waited so long, looking out for you! . . ."

"Exactly as long as I've been watching for you, sparrow! Whenever the rebel army headed over toward our neck of the woods, it had me all atremble. We were camped near Święta Katarzyna, and people were saying we would be moving off in the direction of the Samsonowskie Woods. We veered a little closer to Kostomłoty and Strawczyn, and I couldn't wait any longer. I jumped on my horse and came to see you!"

Szczepan came in. He was told to bring the tall boots. He looked into Mr. Brynicki's face. He stared at him as if he were seeing him for the first time, though they had lived alongside each other for decades.

"What are you looking at?" asked Brynicki. "Look to your work!"

"I do look to my work. As long as there's something to look to."

"Something or other will always be left."

"I can see they won't come plowing this field much longer."

"Maybe they will, maybe they won't. Though it's not clear who 'they' might be. You just wait here!"

"I'm waiting. Pity I'm the last."

"Don't play the wise guy; that's not part of your job. Have I ever wronged you?"

"How would I know who's wronged me? Probably not."

"You'd be better off going and cooking me up something. A nice hunk of fried meat. . ."

The old man gave a painful sigh. "What kind of cook can I be? Will this ever end?"

"Cut the moaning! It'll come to an end," Brynicki said firmly.

"The master and mistress are gone. Is there any news of them?"

"I don't know anything. In the woods only the spruce trees murmur; there's no news to be heard."

Brynicki beckoned and called Szczepan close to him. The two of them went into the hallway, and the steward began whispering loudly in the cook's ear:

"Who's this fellow lying here?"

"Who knows? The young lady calls him 'duke.'"

"I don't know what to think of it. Is he a bad type?"

"He doesn't look like a villain."

"Listen! . . . You know what I'm going to ask you?"

"I do."

"Well then?"

"I don't think he's laid a finger on her."

"Tell me the truth, dammit!"

"I don't know if girls like that can be watched if they take something into their head. Or if she took a fancy to a fellow like that, could anyone do anything about it? But it seems to me as if nothing's going on. I mean, he's lying there like a lump of wood . . . And he's a heavy bastard, too; when I carry him to the barn it's like picking up a stallion. A duke to rebuke!"

"Szczepan!"

"Hm?"

"Mind that child of mine," the old steward hissed in the cook's unhearing ear.

"I've been keeping an eye on that business even without being asked."

"If she makes that choice herself, then we'll have to live with it. But if you ever notice that he's trying to take her by force or by guile, take the last fencepost and smash him over the head with it! No questions asked! Hit him as if you were striking with my hand!"

"All right."

They went back into the cold room, and here Brynicki took pleasure in changing into clean clothes and putting on new boots. Szczepan made some of his everlasting kasha and brought it in. He put a large bowl in the injured man's room and handed out wooden spoons. Then he stepped aside. But Brynicki thrust a spoon into his hand and told him to eat with them. The old cook was embarrassed and tried to refuse. What kind of right did he have to eat supper with the masters! Never were such things—the pig lying down with the swineherd . . . In the end he squatted by the table on which the bowl stood and began solemnly, modestly, almost reverently, eating a little with the masters. The sick duke reached out to the bowl from his bed.

After supper Brynicki lay down to sleep on the couch in the sick man's bedroom. Miss Mija knelt at his pillow. The old man put his arm around his only daughter. They dozed, whispered to each other, fell silent, then went on with their stories of the days and the nights. Advice, suggestions, and requests followed one another . . . They prayed together quietly and profoundly. The old soldier spoke of marches, retreats, camps, and defeats . . . He mentioned places that had been liberally bathed in blood: Wąchock, Suchedniów, Święty Krzyż . . . And then more of the same . . .

The duke listened to his stories and added details about his own unit. They whispered like this through the dark of night. The dawn was approaching when the old gentleman summoned Szczepan and ordered him to bring out the horse, which was feeding in the barn. He put his arms round his daughter, holding her to his heart in a painful, endless embrace. He asked her to carry various bundles and odds and ends outside and to tie them to the saddle. When she had left the room, he reached out and shook hands with the sick man.

"Well, my friend, I have to be going. I wish you good health; God grant that we meet again as free men."

"May God grant that wish!"

"And when you get better, help my child; counsel her, defend her."

The duke nodded.

"And if you should ever harm her," grunted the old man, "then watch out! Because I'll find you, dead or alive."

With these words he walked out. The young woman's soft crying could be heard; then dull, even hoofbeats.

VIII

One day in March, toward evening, a two-horse gig pulled up in front of the veranda at Niezdoły and two travelers climbed out. One of them was around fifty, the other younger. The older man carried a large leather bag slung across his shoulder and was dressed like an itinerant merchant or craftsman. The younger one wore light shoes and town clothes and looked as if he might be his companion's secretary or assistant. The moment the two men stood by the veranda, the gig drove off. No one noticed whose crest it bore. The newcomers entered the manor and, not encountering anyone in the hallway, sat at a table in the first large drawing room.

This all happened so quickly that the occupants of the house had no time to secure the wounded man or to greet or entertain the visitors. It was only after a while that Miss Salomea went out to them. The guests bowed courteously, asked if they could stay the night, and requested a meal and horses for the next day to take them to a destination close by. The young mistress explained that there were no horses and that it would be difficult to provide a meal, since the house had been ransacked of everything. She could only give them a bed for the night, which in fact meant plain bedding on the couch and the sofa in that very room. The visitors bowed again and began asking discreetly about how things stood. Accustomed to bad manners, threats, molestations, and even pushing and raised fists, she was taken aback by this politeness. Under its influence, she announced that she could offer the only dish there was: the daily kasha, which she was growing sick of, yet which was also running low.

The two men continued to ask about everything: the family names and Christian names of the owners of the manor and of its present occupants; details of the plundered property, the burned-down buildings, relations with the farmers and the servants; the passage of the opposing forces, where they camped, and how the Russian army and the Polish insurgents had behaved.

Miss Salomea took a liking to the elder of the two men. He had deep, honest gray eyes, wise beyond words and watchful despite the extreme exhaustion that could be read in his face. His thick, close-cut hair was beginning to turn white. Tall, rawboned, and strongly built, with a slight stoop, he was somehow inexpressibly close to her, like a father or a brother. When, in response to the question about who lived in the manor, she replied that she was alone there with an elderly cook, he was struck by her answer and fell to thinking. Yet he was marked by a calm that was not surprised by anything and was not frightened of anything. It was simply that his eyes became more attentive, better, and more kindly.

The other traveler was noticeably sterner and less patient. He stared at the furniture and into Miss Salomea's eyes mistrustfully, though he was silent and assented to everything. For a long time the first man continued to ask about all kinds of things—so long, in fact, that Miss Brynicka, taught by her father to be cautious and reticent in giving out any sort of information to strangers, began to apply this principle. The older traveler seemed to understand this and to appreciate it, and even to approve of such restraint. He changed his line of questioning.

On the pretext of having to give instructions about the bedding, Miss Salomea left the drawing room, which was lit by the lantern, and entered the darkened bedroom where the wounded man lay. The door was open. Odrowąż called her in a barely audible whisper, inclined her head to his mouth, and, moving his lips almost soundlessly, said into her ear:

"That tall older man in the other room is a leading figure in the uprising. He's a commissioner in the national government. His name is Hubert Olbromski."

Miss Salomea looked round and saw the man's profile by the light of the lantern. He supported his tired head with his hand as he rested his elbow on the table, listening attentively to what the younger man was explaining to him in a whisper.

"What about the other one?"

"I don't know his name, but I've seen his face somewhere. He's also someone important."

"The older one is very nice."

"He's a powerful man."

"Do you know him?"

"His face and his work I know well. I used to see him in Paris."

"What was he doing there?"

"Organizing, traveling as an emissary . . ."

They were whispering as quietly as they could, yet their conversation caught the attention of the two guests. Both fell silent and peered into the darkness. After a moment the younger man took the lantern and moved quickly to the door of the unlit bedroom. He lifted up the light, and they saw the sick man. The younger visitor held a raised pistol.

"Who's that?" he asked sharply.

"I'm an insurgent; my name is Józef Odrową ż."

"Whose regiment are you in?"

"I'm in the cavalry, under Langiewicz."

"What are you doing here?"

"I was wounded at the battle of Małogoszcz. This young lady has kindly allowed me to stay here while I recover."

Olbromski and his companion looked hard into the duke's eyes. They took turns asking him about various details; concluding that he was telling the truth, they muttered something to each other and went back to the drawing room. Without waiting for the kasha that had been promised, they took from their overcoat pockets a bottle of vodka, bread, and cold ham and partook of these supplies. At the same time they asked their young hostess for pen and ink. After a search, she eventually found the items among the abandoned paraphernalia in the house and gave them to the two men.

The two of them set about writing something. The older man dictated, concentrating hard and thinking carefully. The younger one wrote. Then afterward the secretary read back what he had taken down, while Olbromski added notes and comments. Once they had finished, they reviewed various papers, some kind of memoranda or reports; then they traced lines on maps they had unfolded, measuring distances with compasses and listing something in record books. Their eyes were lost in this work; their features became sharp and severe, while their faces conveyed utter and complete engrossment.

When they had completed their work, they carefully examined the doors and windows. The younger man took the lantern and went off to inspect the whole house and the way out through the back of the manor, where they could escape into the garden. Hubert Olbromski sat in the great room. He lit a wax candle that he had in his bag and, leaning his head on his arm, read some document. Miss Brynicka came in to put warmer blankets on their beds. Olbromski spoke to her:

"Excuse me for asking one more question. You mentioned that your name is Brynicka, is that correct?"

"That's right."

"Was there someone in your family who fought in the revolution?"

"My father served as a soldier during the revolution."

"A tall, thick-set man with a drooping mustache? An oval face . . . taciturn fellow by the name of Antoni."

"My father's name is Antoni."

Olbromski smiled. His eyes glazed over. He spoke as if of a trivial, incidental matter:

"You know . . . when I was a little boy of ten, before the last revolution, my father, Rafał, was arrested for involvement in that business long ago with Machnicki.* I was at school, alone in the world, alone in a city that at that time seemed to me to be as big as the whole world. Near my lodgings were the light-horsemen's barracks. I got to know one of the soldiers by the name of Antoni Brynicki. He would come and visit me to cheer me up when my father was locked up in a faraway prison . . . That soldier used to take me to the barracks and let me sit on his horse, and any others that I wanted to. To take my mind off things, he would show me the military equipment: broadswords, carbines, musket balls and powder, cartridge pouches, saddles, bridles, and spurs, . . . He would pick me up and seat me on his lap . . . he would tell me splendid war stories . . . So many years have passed since then! I've been all over and seen all sorts of things; yet I can remember every word of his as if it were yesterday! Where is your father now?"

"In the Polish army."

Olbromski nodded. He asked: "Is he commanding some unit? What's his pseudonym?"

"He's just serving as a regular soldier."

*The reference is to an anticzarist plot of the early 1820s among Polish officers, many of whom were imprisoned or executed for their involvement. One of the leading conspirators was Kazimierz Machnicki (1780–1844), who also played a prominent role in the 1830–31 uprising.—TRANS.

He nodded again and smiled at the young lady.

"And where is your father?" she inquired, emboldened by his good-natured expression.

"My father was killed long ago in the Galician massacre, cruelly murdered near the village of Stokłosy on the Vistula by peasants who had been incited to it.* They sawed him in half alive, after he had returned to those parts all the way from France in order to fight for freedom one more time . . . And I was forced to witness it. That's the tragedy of the Polish gentry," he said with his wise, sorrowful smile.

He turned his head away for a moment. Then he added: "So you're Antoni Brynicki's daughter! I can even see the resemblance in your eyes and in your mouth. He and I were greatly fond of each other in those days, even though he was a big soldier and I was just a little boy in a provincial school."

He reached out his hand, took hers, clasped it, and said: "God grant you happiness, young lady! May He give you all that's good!"

Miss Salomea wanted to thank him for this blessing, but she did not know how. The words stuck in her throat. She raised her grave and fearless eyes to him.

"What is it?" he asked.

"I'm all alone here!" she sobbed. "My father was here a few days ago and then he left once again!"

"Such is fate."

"Such is fate! And who created that fate?"

"Who created it?"

*In 1846 a peasant rebellion in Galicia, the part of Poland occupied by Austria, led to the brutal massacre of hundreds of members of the landed gentry. The Austrian authorities encouraged the rebels, since many of the gentry had been planning their own uprising against the partitioning power.—TRANS.

"You did!"

He looked at her intently and calmly. She felt that she had been not merely extremely rude, but also cruel. Without knowing what she was doing or why, she slipped from her chair to the ground and found herself kneeling at his feet. He tried to help her up, but she seized his hands and gazed deep into his eyes.

"Tell me!" she exclaimed.

"What?"

"What are you doing?"

"What do you mean?"

"This uprising!"

"The uprising."

"Please, explain it to me; use your reason and your conscience. I'm just a simple, foolish woman . . . I can't understand it at all!"

"I'll tell you everything, everything I know."

"On your conscience?"

"On my conscience."

She looked in his eyes and knew that she would hear the truth. She cried defiantly: "Which of you will dare to say that he'll defeat those who come here in the night to torment innocent people like us? And if you can't defeat them, which of you dared to unleash the savagery that they brought here in their souls from the cruel snows? Do you have in yourselves a strength that is equal to their savagery and is capable of crushing that evil?"

Olbromski was silent. She gave a sob and went on with her accusations:

"The Russian soldiers burn down manor houses and kill the wounded on the battlefields. The farmers tie up the insurgents—"

He interrupted her in a different, hard voice: "You prefer their savagery to wounds and death? That savagery will reign over you for all time!"

"It already does, in spite of all the wounds."

"The Polish tribe has found itself between two millstones of destruction: the Germans and Moscow. It must either become a millstone itself or be ground up as fodder for the other two. There is no other choice. Any further discussion is superfluous."

"What can we believe in? What can we live by?"

"Arm yourself with a brave heart."

"What use is a brave heart!" she groaned in despair.

"This is no longer the time for questions and answers."

The younger visitor returned to the drawing room, having checked the buildings, pathways, and bushes around the house. Miss Salomea left immediately. The two officials undressed and went to sleep, each with a loaded gun under his pillow.

The night was quiet, and there was a hint of spring. Mild breaths of wind passed over the earth and seemed to penetrate the living quarters. The sick man was restless. The presence of the two men inhibited him, and his sufferings were thereby intensified. He tossed and turned in his bed, sighing all the while. From the next room could be heard the heavy snoring of the two commissioners. Both were sound asleep.

For a long time Miss Salomea was unable to sleep. A weight lay upon her heart. After her conversation with Olbromski, she missed her father more than ever. An indefinable sorrow gripped her soul, while a nighttime anxiety with no particular cause kept making the hairs on the back of her neck stand on end. Every so often she rose up on her bed to listen intently. This constant nightly waiting for the enemy filled her body and her soul with an aversion for people. She always had to stay on her guard with them, to be on the alert, to watch out for them sneaking up unexpectedly.

That night her unease intensified. She began to be concerned for the older of the two visiting politicians. This man had become dear to her from the moment she had first laid eyes upon him. She was afraid that something untoward might happen to him there. She wished that this interminable night would pass and that the two men would be able to leave on their long journey to a free Poland. She tried to fall asleep but was utterly unable to. At times she trembled like a leaf. Worries assailed her like the sudden ringing of bells.

She strained her ears in mortal torment. It seemed to her that Dominik was walking about the house. Listening closely to the silence, she caught rustling sounds that may well not have existed at all. Something passed like a breeze through the adjoining rooms. Something was sighing . . . In the profound silence something was giving a warning. The old floorboards creaked. A distant snap . . . Was that the creak of one of the doors covered in dried varnish? It was as if someone wanted to shout out but couldn't make a sound. In a moment the barrels would start to crash as they were flung down from high up onto the floor . . .

She leaned on her elbow and listened.

Even the wounded insurgent had fallen fast asleep. The two visitors were silent in their speechless slumber . . .

Her eyes, staring into the void, seemed to make out Dominik's face. He stood in the open door with his hand to his mouth, as if he were stifling a cry. He didn't want to cry out, and he wasn't able to leave. A cold draft passed through the room, blowing her hair back from her forehead and making her flesh crawl.

She covered her head with her shawl and her eyes with her hair and, horrified, hid her face in her pillow so as not to see. Then sleep came to her unexpectedly and gave her a few hours of blessed respite. She sank completely, as if into the bottomless abyss of darkness. A moment ago she had rested her forehead on her pillow and covered it up so as not to see the apparition; then it had been the middle of the night, but now her eyes opened to see a bright morning. The white square of the window in the gray room . . . the canary singing an early morning song . . . What was that? A banging sound! Dominik was hurling down the vats! Another bang! Another! Lord save us!

She opened her eyes and sat up in bed. Another bang! She shook herself and realized what was going on. They were hammering with rifle butts at the three front windows! At the door! She leaped to her feet and staggered as if she were drunk. What was she to do? Whom should she call? Everyone was asleep! The banging came from every side of the manor. There came a familiar cry that chilled the blood in her veins and the marrow in her bones, shouting in Russian:

"*Otpiray!* Open up!"

The door from the kitchen opened. Szczepan hurried in on tiptoe, pallid, quaking, terrified, and in a panic. He nudged Miss Salomea and pointed at the insurgent. Then he rushed into the large drawing room and set about bestirring the overnight visitors. He tugged at their hair with both hands and beat on their chests with his fists. He shook their heads with all his might. At last he managed to wake them both. They jumped up and listened. The pounding at the door finally brought them to their senses.

In a moment they pulled on their trousers and shoes. The younger one threw on his jacket. The older man could not find his coat and had just slipped the leather bag over his shoulder when the shutter was torn off, the window was broken and fell with a crash, and soldiers began to clamber one after another into the room. All the entrances were blocked. A clattering could be heard everywhere. Szczepan led the commissioners as quickly as possible in the opposite direction, toward Dominik's apartment. He opened the door and shoved both of them in.

They rushed across the large room with the barrels and ran into the next one. They opened the window quietly. At that place the house had a tall foundation half the height of a normal story. When they opened the shutters, which were locked from the inside, they saw two soldiers who were just clambering up to reach the window frame. Olbromski and his companion took cover against the wall and cocked their pistols in readiness.

Szczepan had left them and run back to the bedroom. He and Miss Salomea carried the wounded duke on his mattress through the small hallway and lowered him into one of the great vats in the former drawing room. When they had done this, they both took refuge in Dominik's room. Here they saw the younger visitor still poised behind the window, lying in wait for the soldiers. Suddenly a Russian helmet appeared in the window frame and a soldier came through the opening. The moment his head passed through the window, Olbromski's companion put the pistol to his forehead and shot him between the eyes. The soldier crashed down on his back. A second shot felled the other dragoon.

In the meantime, the manor was in an uproar; the soldiers crashed about and shouted as they searched the house. They had broken in through the doors and the windows. The visitors had to escape. Their path clear after the two soldiers had fallen, Olbromski and his comrade climbed out of the window and, holding on to the frame, let themselves down the rough wall to the ground.

At the entrance to the courtyard, about fifteen horses belonging to the dragoons storming the manor were tied up by the broken gate. These horses were being guarded by a single soldier who was still in the saddle. Olbromski's companion rushed full tilt toward these horses and the soldier. He pulled a second pistol from his belt, and from no more than a couple of paces he shot and wounded the rider, incapacitating him. Then, all at once, he leaped into the saddle of the closest mount, untied the reins from the post, turned the horse around, and, striking it with all his strength left and right with the strap of the bridle, hurtled out of the gateway.

Olbromski had cleared the fence and was about to follow suit, but he was too late. The soldiers had heard the shots and had seen from the window what had happened. They ran for their horses and cut him off. He jumped over another broken-down fence and rushed headlong downhill through the garden that led toward the river.

Miss Salomea was standing in the window and saw both incidents, which happened ten times faster than they can be told. She gripped the window frame and watched the younger man on the dragoon's horse racing down the road to the bridge in a flurry of splashing mud and melted snow. He crossed the bridge, rode out into the fields, and thundered across the low-lying meadows at an ever-increasing gallop. He leaned over and lay flat on the horse's neck so that he could barely be seen. As his stallion galloped along at breakneck speed, it became ever lower and longer. He flew over the even ground like some great bizarre bird. Six dragoons had chased off after him. Little puffs of blue smoke kept bursting over their heads. They were firing at the man who was escaping, but to no avail, as he galloped on and on toward the woods. Eventually he disappeared from view.

Miss Salomea leaned out of the window, looking for the older man. But Szczepan prized her fingers from the frame and dragged the distracted woman behind him. Nor did he allow her to stop by the hidden insurgent. They hurried as fast as possible out through the hallway and the door, which had been abandoned by the soldiers, slipped unseen through the garden, and ran up the hill. Szczepan was running away like a little boy now; he muttered something to himself and pulled Miss Salomea after him. He crouched like a fox behind one of the larger juniper bushes and instructed her to do the same. Peeping out from behind the bush, they observed what was going on.

Through the leafless trees, in the mild light of morning, they watched a terrible thing happen by the river. There were shouts and brutish cries . . . Miss Mija held her breath. Her hands convulsively grasped hold of the juniper branches with their sharp needles. Her body swayed. She fainted. Szczepan brought her round by rubbing her temples with handfuls of the blackened snow that still lurked underneath the coarse bush.

In the meantime, along the riverbank Hubert Olbromski was fighting his last heroic battle. Vesnitsyn, the same dragoon officer who had searched the manor once before and who burned with a savage love for Miss Salomea, had received orders to pursue two commissioners of the Polish National Government and had tracked them from place to place until he had caught up with them here. From the veranda he had watched one of them escape on a horse belonging to the dragoon unit. He had orders to take both of them alive as they slept somewhere. He had followed his instructions to the letter. He had come at exactly the right time. For this reason he harbored a passionate desire to capture the other man, at least. As he raced down toward the river behind the soldiers, he yelled at the top of his lungs:

"Keep him alive! Take him alive! Only alive! Don't you dare open fire! Take him with your bare hands! Hold him! Surround him!"

Olbromski heard these shouted commands. He sensed death in his heart. Round his neck he bore his bag, which contained all his documents, including thousands of secrets of the Polish government, concerning everything that had happened and that might come to pass. It was as if he carried in that bag the heart of fighting Poland, in which a living blood flowed. He wasn't able to hide the bag anywhere, or to abandon it as he ran, or to destroy it, since ten soldiers were chasing after him. He fled in leaps and bounds. He vaulted over bushes, rotten fences, muddy strips of cultivated land, a ditch that was still iced over.

He reached the meadows. He noticed something like a thicket and raced off in that direction. But all at once terror struck him like fire. Out of the blue he saw the river before him. Swollen from the spring thaw and the rains until it had reached the top of its banks, filled with whirling, bubbling black water that swept past, it blocked his path with a half-circle to the left and another to the right. Its wordless murmur struck the fugitive's ear, while his frantic eyes beheld its serpentine blackness like an accursed, derisive power that had cut off his last escape route. His quick thinking had slipped up; his last hope for deliverance had failed. His eyes were blinded by a dark despair.

Then the inscrutable, swirling current opened its black waters as if it were opening its heart. He understood and uttered a moan. He pulled the strap from his shoulder and hurled the leather bag with the secrets of Poland far out into the water. The river gave a splash like a sign or a mute reply and closed up, folding in a thousand waves the treasure that had been entrusted to it. Then it continued on its long journey, winding, ancient, and yet ever new. The man sighed. The soldiers had seen what he had done. They caught up with him and encircled him on all sides. He turned to face them. Lieutenant Vesnitsyn was running up behind them, still calling:

"Take him alive! Alive! Don't you dare kill him. Surround him!"

Olbromski took strength. He scorned a lengthy prison sentence or death on the gallows. He took his stand. When the first of the Russian soldiers drew near to him, he shot him in the head with his pistol. He seized the saber that fell from the dead man's hand and struck another soldier in the neck with all his might. With his left hand he pulled another pistol from his belt and downed his next attacker. Behind him was the river; before him seven assailants. He fought like a cornered tiger.

The soldiers heard their commanding officer's incessant orders to take him alive and barely even used their swords. They advanced on him all together with bare hands. He took advantage of the order and slashed out, hacking for all he was worth, thrusting at them as he edged along the bank, looking for a place where he could jump into the water and escape to the other bank. The officer saw that three dragoons had fallen and that those remaining were having difficulty handling this one man; he moved forward with his saber drawn. Olbromski noticed him beyond the ring of soldiers and shouted at him contemptuously:

"You! You coward!"

The sullen officer's blood began to boil. He leaped into the circle of dragoons, gripping his sword and intending to knock the commissioner's saber from his hand. The two blades clashed like lightning once and twice.

Olbromski took his pistol by the barrel and smashed it over the head of a soldier who was trying to grab his arm during the fight. With his sword he struck the officer's shoulder and hit the soldier to his right-hand side between the eyes.

"Take him!" roared the officer.

They surged forward. He swung out left and right. He got away from them, drawing them after him. He lashed out into the crowd. The enraged lieutenant sliced at his neck with his saber, then cut his face. This unleashed the soldiers' fury. They forgot about their orders. They rushed at their prey and swung at his head with their swords, hacking at his throat with random blows. Olbromski dropped his weapon; he staggered and fell. They belabored his skull until his brains spurted out and spattered on the grass. They chopped at his arms, his breast, and his ribs. As he lay on the ground they hacked his belly and his legs until every last drop of blood had been spilled. It flowed from his veins, soaked into the meadow, and was drunk by the soft, thirsty spring earth.

Vesnitsyn, the great dark officer, looked down upon him with a lofty frown as he slipped his greasy, bloodied saber back into its scabbard. He had avenged himself as a soldier, but he had failed to carry out his superiors' orders. He ordered the dragoons to begin immediately to search the river for the rebel's leather bag. But the water was deeper than the height of a man and icy cold, and the current was rapid. The first soldier who slipped off his boots, undressed, and plunged into the waters at once turned numb with cold. The same happened to the second and the third. Then they tried searching by plumbing the riverbed over and again with poles, still to no avail.

The officer then instructed them to round up all the men from the village and, first issuing an order, then later promising a substantial reward, told them to use any and all means to find the leather bag belonging to the dead *myatezhnik.** A few dozen farmers were brought together on the riverbank; they thought long and hard, discussed the problem in great depth, and offered each other and the soldiers a series of invaluable pieces of advice and wise observations. They argued fiercely about a plan of action, shaking their fists at each other. The river, begging the lieutenant's pardon, was ever so deep; there were terrible troughs in it, while along the banks there were extensive snags, and on the bottom lay roots and boulders that had been there since time immemorial, when floods had brought them there from God knows where. Then the current was swift, cold, evil . . .

A few of them volunteered to go in up to their necks and wade

**Myatezhnik* is Russian for "rebel."—TRANS.

along the banks; immediately afterward they hopped out and scuttled off to the village, shaking with cold, their teeth chattering.

Others brought fishing nets and used them to trawl the deep waters over a long stretch downstream. Others still moved from place to place, poking in the water with rods and boat hooks. This went on until midday. It was all in vain.

The river did not give up the secret that had been entrusted to it. The dragoon officer returned from the riverbank to the manor in an ominous frame of mind. He ordered the village clerk immediately to provide several horses and carts to transport the wounded soldiers to the town. He had two corpses, three severely wounded men, and two with less serious injuries. In addition, he had lost a horse. He had fought with two leading figures in the uprising whom he had had orders to capture alive. One of them had escaped with his life; the other had been killed without giving up any information about himself. And above all, the documents that the dead man had had in his hands were lost, sunk without trace in the river.

The officer was shaken to the limits of despair. On pain of the most terrible punishment, he forbade the farmers to bury the dead rebel. He gave orders that he should rot where he lay in the meadow and that the birds should peck him to pieces before the eyes of the whole village. When the dead and wounded soldiers had been loaded onto the carts lined with straw, and the caravan of vehicles had slowly pulled away, the lieutenant ordered one group of his men to give the horses some hay in the barn and another detachment to search the manor, the courtyard, the garden, the cellars, and the immediate surroundings of the outbuildings.

He felt the need to vent his rage upon someone and to take revenge for such a disastrous failure. He wanted to have in his clutches the young woman who lived in this house and whom he had never been able to forget through all the most terrible events of those times. After all, she was the one who had harbored two of the leaders of the conspiracy. As irrefutable proof of her guilt, the men's bedding still lay in the large drawing room.

The scowling officer walked right through the completely deserted manor himself and checked in cubbyholes, in side rooms, in the hallways, and on the stairs. As he passed from room to room, he found himself in the great drawing room with the containers from the distillery; from there he walked through into the next chamber, where the legendary Dominik had lived and from where that morning the two conspirators had jumped through the window into the garden. The room was long and devoid of furniture. It seemed to invite one to pace across it. Lieutenant Vesnitsyn wished to be alone. Without any awareness of what he was doing, he began to wander from corner to corner.

Cruel thoughts and monstrous feelings heaped down upon his head. This abandoned, ruined house reminded him of his family home in the depths of Russia. The events that had just taken place, with the chase and the fight with the two insurgents, set all the incidents of the war in a particular light. And at the bottom of it all lay a blind desire for vengeance, an inconsolable torment that arose from unrequited love. The lieutenant despised himself . . . The other man, surrounded by soldiers and standing in his shirtsleeves on the steep riverbank, had called out a word that had struck him like the blow of a knout. This word enraged him and seared into his very core. For that word the man had lost his life and had been left on the meadow for the crows to peck at.

Yet another word stirred in his memory and cawed at him like the scavenging birds sitting on a corpse. It was a phrase from an article by Herzen* that had been aimed at the Russian soul: "Leave there at once, or you'll be pecking at our own dead like a crow . . ." A deep laugh, like someone's inner laughter, rang in his breast: *Kluy voronom nashi trupy . . .*

These were not words; they were the image of blood dripping from a naked sword. Their meaning was composed of the memory of what had occurred, dried into a dark red mass. As he strode about the room, the young dragoon cursed with the worst invectives in the Russian language; he strained like a wolf on a leash and from time to time sobbed inwardly without shedding any tears. It was no time ago that he had been sitting with a circle of friends, reading the brilliant émigré's lofty vituperations. Not only did he take these to heart and breathe them; he joined the ranks of those men. Now, "out of a sense of duty" he was pecking out the eyes of the dead. He knew that nothing in him could resist the feeling of duty that had been forged in the Russian soul by the centuries, on the executioner's block. He wept.

The bare walls of the room seemed to drive despair into his heart and to set the poison of death in his veins. There was something here that mocked the self-assurance of a brutal power, its strength and its unleashing, healthy bodies and the lives of beings. Something here kept company with the human visitor—something that was like him and yet was entirely other; it walked with him in his solitude, a nonexistent shadow, and stared with the putrefying eyes of a corpse at his living feelings, at his courageous agony, his tribulations that cried out for revenge.

When the lieutenant looked behind him, he saw only the old dirt and rubbish on the floor, a thick covering of dust that stretched

*Alexander Herzen (1812–70) was a Russian émigré political writer who opposed the czarist regime; he came out in support of the Polish uprising of 1863–64.—TRANS.

into corners where no foot had stepped for years. The sight of this dust did not calm him; it agitated him further. He searched it for the footprints of the man who had not been able to win the fight in his lifetime and who had continued to struggle with life after his own death. On his previous visits Lieutenant Vesnitsyn had heard the legend of Dominik. Now he had it and felt it within himself. He was enfolded, taken into the embrace of an overpowering world-weariness, an abhorrence for all he had done and all that he would do, and an understanding of the futility of all that was courage and strength of character, military genius and conscious action in this war. After so many mortifications and so many actions, his hands were empty, and within him he had not so much a feeling soul as the howling of a wolf in the wilderness. After all the heroism, the strife, the labors, and the sleeplessness, the Russian question was staring him in the eyes: What was it all for?

As he was pacing from corner to corner of Dominik's room, he heard a soft, protracted moan. He could not tell where it came from. He stopped in his tracks and listened intently. The moaning was repeated, lingering in an unbearable monotone. The officer realized that the sound was coming from the next room. He crept in on tiptoe and came to the source of the noise. Taking hold of the rim of the vat, he hoisted himself up athletically and looked down inside the huge container. From its depths the insurgent's eyes stared up at him, burning like flames. The dragoon sat on the rim, brought his legs over, and jumped down into the vat. He laughed with a coarse pleasure. At last he had found something with which he could suppress his despondency and with a single blow put an end to the tumult in his soul.

He pulled his pistol from his belt and placed the muzzle between the eyes of the man who lay there.

"Who are you?" he asked.

"An insurgent," replied Odrowąż.

"How did you end up here?"

"I'm wounded."

"Where did that happen?"

"In battle."

"Where are your wounds?"

"I have a bullet wound in my hip."

"Who hid you here?"

The duke said nothing. Vesnitsyn nodded; he understood. His eyes filmed over with rage. He asked: "Did the young lady hide you here?"

The duke remained silent.

"I arrest you!" said Vesnitsyn.

"What for? Kill me. You have a loaded pistol in your hand. If you're a soldier, if you're an officer, then shoot me! After all, you people know how to murder the wounded."

Vesnitsyn stared him in the eyes; he held his cocked gun loosely in his hand. He found this Polish courage repugnant. He muttered: "Stand up! I arrest you!"

"If you take me away from here, I'll die on the way. If I survive, when I'm in prison I won't tell you anything. I'm just a rank-and-file soldier. Shoot me!"

"I'll do as I wish."

"If you don't shoot me, then you'll have acted like a coward!"

"Quiet!"

"If I could stand, I'd kill you like a dog! So you kill me like a dog! We're mortal enemies."

"You're not an enemy worthy of me, you slave."

"I want my suffering to end at last. Oh! . . ."

"Lie where you are, lover boy."

The officer sank deep in thought as he stood over this man. Should he raise his hand and shoot him between the eyes? Should he walk away? His inner torment intensified. That mockery once again . . . He turned his back in disgust; he seized hold of the edge of the vat, pulled himself up, and jumped out.

The detachment of soldiers who had been chasing the insurgent on horseback was just returning. They came back on sweating, steaming horses spattered with yellow foam; but they were empty-handed. The sergeant major reported that the rebel on the dragoon's sorrel had reached a wood, had ridden off the road as far as they could tell, and afterward must have zigzagged across moss and grass, because they lost the trail at this point. They had split up and combed the wood from one end to the other. They searched in all directions but had been unable to find his tracks again.

The soldiers who had gone looking for the young woman also returned with nothing. They had asked people in the village, had spied and hunted; but she must have gotten far away . . .

The officer heard out both reports in gloomy silence. He felt for this manor the same abhorrence one feels for old graves. It was all the same to him whether he shot the insurgent between his blazing eyes or whether he rode off to the distant woods. He reflected for a moment. He ordered his men to bridle the horses and to mount up and prepare to leave. But he still lingered on the veranda. He was waiting. He longed for the beautiful young lady to return. He wished to make her a gift—to tell her, with that inner smile, that he was leaving the man in the vat as a present for her. He had seen him, and yet he had not killed him, nor had he taken him away. He wanted to see in her eyes a glimmer of gratitude, a spark of emotion, the pallor of fear, the flush of shame, a human glance . . . Nothing suggested that she would appear, but he waited with the confidence known only to those in love.

The soldiers had long been seated in the saddle. He jumped onto his horse. His eyes closed, he rode off, with night in his soul and with an inconceivable cry in that night.

IX

Toward evening, several hours after the dragoons had disappeared into the woods, Miss Salomea and Szczepan returned to the manor from their hiding place on the hill. The two of them ran to the wounded man, lifted him from the vat, and laid him back in bed. They also went at once down to the river. So much blood had run from Olbromski's body that all the earth around him was sodden.

Miss Salomea knelt by the dead man. She was unable to cry. The man who yesterday had looked upon her with kind, intelligent eyes, the only man she would have trusted, now lay disfigured, cut to pieces. She understood neither the sequence of events, nor the way what had happened had been determined by deep-rooted causes, nor the fearful chaos that spun her about like a drop of water in a mill wheel. She did not realize that she herself was a small part of why that mill wheel turned. Her father, a simple, loyal soldier, had not been able to explain all this to her; nor could the insurgent, a simple volunteer, or any of the people who passed through the house, which had come to resemble a public building.

She sensed that some people had flung themselves into the turmoil of the struggle out of a fanaticism that knew no measure and no limits; others were driven by faulty logic; others still because they were ordered to, for fashion, following the herd; and yet others out of cowardice, because they were afraid of public opinion. That one man, her guest from the day before, knew what all the chaos meant; he had measured its power, calculated its direction, and set it on a path that he alone knew. He would have explained it all to her; he would have taught her the meaning of these events, for wisdom and justice shone in his eyes like stars in the night. Yet he was the very one who lay at her feet, his head cut open and his brains hacked out by a naked sword.

She was unable to cry. She was choking from something that blocked her throat. She ordered Szczepan to fetch a shovel and dig the man a grave. The old cook sat on the rotten stump of a willow, chewing a hunk of black army bread that he had found left behind on the kitchen table. When she repeated her instructions he began muttering:

"So now I have to dig! All I ever hear is carry this, move that, serve so-and-so or clean up after him! Now it's dig a grave!"

"Be quiet! Look at him . . ."

"Why would I want to do that?"

"Szczepan!"

"Fellows like him run wild whenever they feel like it. They don't do any real work. And now you're telling me to make a grave for him!"

"Quiet now!"

"I'm not the one who's shouting. Don't I always do what needs to be done?"

"If you won't do it, I'll dig him a grave myself."

"The shovel's over there."

A moment later he rose from the stump and began to study a place on a small hillock nearer the house. He pushed the shovel into the soft earth with his foot. He marked out a man-sized area on the grass. Then he spat on his hands and set about digging a hole. He worked in silence and with utter indifference. Throughout all this time Miss Brynicka sat at the dead man's head. She didn't notice the farmers from the village and their women and children coming out from round the corner of the barn and from among the trees. They gathered in small groups, whispering to each other. A circle of curious spectators formed. Szczepan dug a shallow pit. Dusk was falling when he came up, took the corpse by the legs, and dragged it to the grave. Miss Salomea followed behind the body. It was laid in the damp, waterlogged ground and hurriedly covered with black clumps of earth.

The two of them returned slowly to the manor. Their footsteps were heavy, and their hearts dulled and devoid of warmth. They looked with aversion at the dark roof that covered their abode of misery. They crossed the threshold reluctantly. When they came in, their first job was to clear away the bedding of the two visitors from the previous night, which still lay in the large drawing room. Miss Salomea lit the lantern and set to work. Yet when she went up and took hold of the sheets, she was filled with disgust. Both sets of bedding were crawling with lice. They had been brought here from Jewish inns, from farmers' couches, from workmen's camps, a sign of how Polish leaders wasted away in the squalid hovels of Poland . . . The lice had remained alive while the two men had disappeared like shadows . . .

X

It was halfway through April. The long winter, which had kept returning, had finally begun to let up. Springtime torrents rushed down from the hill behind the manor, where patches of snow still lurked in the bushes. Braids of water interwove into streams that shone in the sun as they flowed over the sandy slopes of the garden. The fences, railings, flower beds, and hoed paths were ruined, and the spring waters took possession of the hillside, turning it imperceptibly into a desert. A previously nonexistent watercourse now ran at an angle across the garden toward the river. Only the manor stood in its way. Young grass grew everywhere.

During this time the young insurgent's condition improved. A huge abscess formed near the knee of the wounded leg, and a couple of weeks later, one night it burst as if broken open by the injured man's spasmatic cries. The three of them were amazed to see a lead bullet emerge from the swelling! After this Odrową ż became himself again, though he had lost a lot of weight and was still extremely weak. The wounds on his head and body had healed. The cut beneath his eye had mended, and the eye itself was completely unharmed. A thick growth of hair covered the scars on his head. The duke was able to get out of bed and could limp off on his own when he had to go and hide in the barn to avoid the Russian army as it passed through. He also hobbled about the house, with the aid of a walking stick.

One spring day he and Miss Salomea were standing in the window of the bedroom. Pupinetti was singing, his head cocked; as he saw the sun bursting forth from behind the spring clouds, his song grew louder. Outside the window, on the once bare earth a bright grass was growing, a thousand young blades glittering in the fires of spring. In the middle of the lawn there was a slim birch sapling, which was soon to become a tree yet was still frail and thin. Its boughs, top, and sides were covered with delicate balls of fresh, coiled leaves. Through this transparent coating every branch and every twig, every shoot and every stem, was visible. The birch stood in its spring mantle like an angel that had descended from the passing clouds and was resting awhile on this wretched earth.

The streams that ran here and there across the garden covered over the former paths, washed away borders, and destroyed everything that human will and human thought had marked on that sloping ground. An irrepressible joy, the delight of existence at play, pulsed in the sudden twists and turns of the torrents, which gushed headlong toward the lowlands. One of these streams snaked across the former pathways and flowed over the lawn where the bright birch sapling stood. The water silted up the grass, covering it with a yellow film of foreign clay that it had brought from up on the hill. The birch sapling drank from this cold water, and a curious smile spread from it to the stream and united them both.

The same smile appeared on the faces of Duke Odrowąż and Miss Salomea. They reveled in the sight of the young tree and the rushing water. After so many weeks of torment, for the first time they breathed freely and joyfully. It was finally the end of the harsh winter, whose atrocities they had experienced to the full. The wind blew warm again, and the dead earth released its life-giving juices. The winter that had passed seemed like a yawning chasm filled with darkness, like a time that had never existed. They gazed at the grass and the clouds and turned their eyes on each other.

"I wonder whether Dominik sees the spring?" asked Miss Salomea, addressing the garden more than her companion.

"There is no Dominik," he replied.

"Oh, sure there isn't! I've seen him myself."

"It was a dream, like when I was sick."

"Your sickness was a dream, too?"

"A bad dream."

"And the bullet that came out of your wound? Was that also a dream? Oh yes—I wanted to ask you for something . . ."

"Ask me for something? 'Half my kingdom is yours!'"

"Actually, it was only the bullet, though I would like all of it. Will you give me it?"

"Of course."

"Thank you."

"But what will you do with it?"

"What can anyone do with a bullet? I'll fight with it."

"Who with?"

"It's not as if I had any shortage of enemies."

"What enemies would those be?"

"I hardly know where to begin."

"Name me just one!"

"Before long you'll disappear, the way everything disappears around here. Since I'm going to be all alone, I'll think that you were a dream, too; then I'll look at the bullet and I'll know that you really were here."

Odrowąż was silent. His head rested weakly against the window frame. He lapsed into thought. He had suffered so many indescribable, detestable things in this small room, in this house that, like Poland, had no master; yet now, at the idea she had brought up that he would have to "disappear," to go away, his heart was torn by some unknown instrument that caused a ruthless pain a hundred times worse than all the physical agony he had borne. Without moving his head from the window frame, he looked askance at Miss Salomea. After all those trials and tribulations, sleepless nights and privations, she was as fresh as a daisy. The first spring breeze that had touched her pale face had painted it with the subtlest of pink hues and had delicately gilded her forehead and neck. Her teeth, white as the purest cloud in April, smiled between her crimson lips. Shaking her head, she said:

"The Jews from the inn have found out that there's someone at the manor. Ryfka warned me. Some of the villagers saw you limping to the barn. Your presence here is compromising me."

"In a political sense."

"Not only that."

"In a few days I'll slip away and rejoin the rebel army, and everything will be over."

"I see you're itching to be slipping away. And is Your Grace able to walk straight on his own two feet? Because at the convent they taught me a little ditty that went: 'Learn to walk before you fly . . .' "*

"A moment ago you were trying to get rid of me yourself."

"Get rid of you! I'm just wondering what to do next . . ."

"About what?"

"Everything."

"I don't understand."

"What do you need to understand for? You were here, and now you're going to get up and go away. You have more important things on your mind than all this."

"All what?"

"Oh, stop asking so many questions! Everyone's always asking me questions: who, what, how, when, in which way? Make your mind up! I've been bothered almost to death! Do you understand? Give me some advice as well!"

All that Miss Salomea said was as it were the outer letters of words that masked what was within her soul. For a long time now she had sensed a mysterious inner change. She was not her old self.

*The quotation is from the poem "Two Turtles" by Ignacy Krasicki (1735–1801).—TRANS.

She had ceased to be a free young girl. It seemed as if everything were normal and in order; everything was as it should be. The bloody soldier had come and been taken care of, and he would return to his arduous duties in the army. What could be simpler? Yet at the thought of his going away she found herself faced with something that was more terrible than all the sufferings she had been through, something worse than death itself.

Miss Mija kept turning over in her mind the thought that as soon as this Odrowąż had gone, she should do something to hasten her own death. She should think up some action that in itself would be a sufficient reason to be put to death. To be left alone once again in this empty place, with the shade that roamed through it, with the deaf, sullen Szczepan! To wait once again by night for manifestations of the tragedy that continually repeated itself: the nocturnal intrusions, the searches, the abuse . . . Though it was so hard to prove, the vision of those future days was a thousand times more horrible than sudden death.

Her one regret was for her father. How would it be when he came back one night on his wayworn pony, knocked on the window, and heard no reply? He would ride back, and just as he had lived for the heroic, hopeless cause of Poland, so he would die for it. She wished at least to afford him the small comfort of coming to an end that he would approve of: that was, by offering up her life. And she imagined magnificent deeds bathed in a lugubrious charm. She saw these deeds as if they were real, and she grew to know them.

Odrowąż did not exist in any of this. Only from time to time did she remember that it would all be because of him and in his absence. For this reason she felt resentment toward him rather than any other emotion. She heaped various reproaches on his head, and in her dealings with him she was always brusque and sometimes offensive. Yet in secret, how she adored watching him, especially as he slept! He had long hair that hung down in black strands like exquisite feathers; his features were clean-cut and darkened only by a youthful stubble. For a long time now, when he had felt physical pain she had suffered with him, or rather ten times more than him, suffering for his sake to redeem his torments. His wounds had been in her body and in her soul, in her heart and in her dreams. How often had those dreams been visited by his unhearing, sightless wounds like bloody, misshapen phantoms!

Many times she had seen him naked and had been enchanted by the shameless beauty of his manly figure. While his wounds healed and he grew visibly more handsome, the secret seed of his charm grew in her heart. As he returned to consciousness, he became himself again and regained his blue-blooded preferences, dislikes, tastes, and good and bad habits. She absorbed every one of his reactions like an inviolable canon. She liked what he liked and hated anything that he found in the least unpleasant. She could do nothing to please him, to provide for his aristocratic needs; so she persevered in passive waiting. But every step she took, every movement, thought, every feeling and intention, was at his request and for his sake.

She did not want him to know about this. She was ashamed of her feelings as of a mortal sin. She concealed them from him and covered them with an external asperity; but this only intensified her inner torment and confusion.

Previously they had slept in the same room together. When the nights were no longer so cold, she took her bedding through into the large drawing room. Before she felt the way she did now, she had been able to sleep in that room alongside the wounded man and had been entirely indifferent to the opinion of anyone who might find out. Now that she had this irrepressible, indestructible fear that he would leave, she was ashamed to be with him at night—ashamed before people who were absent and saw nothing, and even before herself.

Yet it was true that within her there was a smoldering desire to kiss his sweet lips and his sorrowful eyes where shadows lurked. Often at night she deliberately left the lantern by his bed, and then, tiptoeing up from the other room to the door of the bedroom, she would gaze endlessly upon those lips and those eyes beneath their lids. There was a mortal bliss in the way her eyes were lost in his lips.

Her mouth was no stranger to kisses. She had been brought up in a house where there were many growing boys—cousins, relatives—and the beautiful young lady was forever a source of temptation to them all. She was not always able to fend off all the various advances and flirtations, and as she yielded to them, she herself grew to know the treacherous power of lingering glances, the first hints of attraction, the pleasures of encounters in darkened rooms and impetuous kisses on the face and neck, which were ostensibly stolen by force yet in reality were offered up voluntarily.

But none of the temporarily lucky fellows possessed Miss Mija's heart. This was more the mischief of a beautiful girl whose successes had caused her to run wild, a fugue played by a stern yet exuberant nature. One older cousin who had stayed at Niezdoły for some time she found attractive as a man. He was more elegant and polite than the others, and most important of all he was handsome. She even yielded to his requests and twice visited him in his guest room. The first time she allowed him to kiss her hands; the second, to put his arms round her and kiss her cheeks and her neck. Yet later, when she noticed that her cousin paid court to any good-looking member of the opposite sex, she regretted her decision, and the whole business left her with a profound feeling of distaste. When her cousin went away, she forgot about him.

Social life and relations between the sexes at Niezdoły Manor were not exactly characterized by subtlety. It was the life of well-to-do gentry with less-than-refined manners. Conversations were banal, while relations with the fair sex were almost vulgar. In this way

Miss Mija had acquired a lot of information from the servants, mostly from conversations among the men, regarding sexual life. Her thoughts had remained at the level of Niezdoły.

It was only now, in her dealings with Duke Odrową ż, that she noticed something different: an exceptional gentleness in the way she was treated, courtesy, cleanliness, and moderation of speech, despite the fact that their life together was so close and out of necessity so immediate. She knew virtually nothing about his relations with his family. During his illness, from the shouts he emitted in pain and his feverish utterances, she concluded that he had a mother. Another time, in a lucid moment he mentioned that he had been educated in Paris and had lived there for an extended period of time. And from a variety of different details she concluded that he must be rich and that he had joined the uprising against the will of his immediate family. All these circumstances surrounded him with an aura of fascination, the irresistible scent of attraction.

When she had to leave the convalescent's room, she was instantly seized with an invincible longing. As soon as she was able to go back there, she was carried in as if by the wind. Now that he had begun to regain his health, his strength awoke in her body. Her concern for his safety also grew stronger. Her entire soul was filled with changes, emotions, and unexpected passions that rose from the depths of her heart; most of all, it was taken up with an unthinking distraction.

On that spring day everything became close and clear. The breeze seemed to draw words from tightly closed lips, to bear them up, and to utter sounds that had been wanting in stifled breasts. The duke was half lying on the windowsill, leaning against the frame, and gazing at the destruction in the garden. He smiled gently and said:

"If it wasn't for you, Miss Salomea, I'd already be lying in that damp earth. The fresh grass would be growing over me."

"At least you'd be of some use that way. As it is, you're nothing but trouble."

"For sure. At least some Russian horse would bite at me and eat me. While as it is, I really am nothing but trouble. Though I did ask several times to be put out of my misery. No one would do it. Not even the dragoon officer . . ."

"You're obviously destined for a higher cause."

"A higher cause made out of wood."

"We're back to that again, are we! Still talking about that triumphal gate of yours . . ."

"Me? Not a word of it!"

"All those princesses would be crying their eyes out if they knew how you had been boiled dry in a vat! It's just as well they'll never find out, or you would drown in a flood of tears."

"What must hang will never drown."*

"Back to the gallows, are we? Somehow death hasn't taken you away yet, so what will be will be, and it won't be the gallows."

"If you'll always protect me from death, then death will do nothing to me."

"Always! That 'always' of yours is only going to last another couple of days, a week or so at the most. How will I be able to save you once you go?"

"Somehow you keeping driving me away with your words."

"Naturally. That's just the kind of inhospitable hostess I am. The larder's so empty that the only thing left to eat is the walls. And all of a sudden I have an unexpected guest—and a duke at that . . ."

Odrowąż raised his heavy head, turned, and looked away. She knew full well that grave tears were falling from his eyes onto the peeling window ledge. She felt a lump in her throat. Her own

*This is a Polish proverb.—TRANS.

thoughtless words cut into her breast like the teeth of a saw. She gave a caustic smile, and looked at him helplessly, not having a clue what to do. Then, against her will, when the hair on her forehead seemed about to burst into flames from her clamorous emotions, she rested her hand on his shoulder. Once she had put it there, she realized that she could not remove it.

She shook his arm lightly. He did not turn his head. Tears were still welling in his eyes. Then, unable to control herself, she raised her trembling hand and stroked his long, black, shining hair. She comforted him as she would an unhappy child, softly whispering quiet, anxious words. Finally she leaned forward and, all transformed into a smile, began to kiss his pale forehead. She kissed it gently, delicately, as if it were a flower that one could never tire of gazing upon or of smelling, and which in the end drew one's lips to itself. With an oblivious love, her lips passed over the strands of his hair.

For a long while he did not turn his head, neither taken aback nor perturbed by her crime. His heart was lost in the depths of sorrow and was neither surprised nor gladdened. When he raised his eyes, they were still filled with tears. He looked at her through those unceasing tears, weeping at the terrible fate of his country and at the defeats whose memory made the blood run cold in his veins . . . He spoke to her of the forces that had been expected and how they had let them down, of the faith and hope that had left only despair behind. She cradled his head close to hers and whispered joyful things in his ears and in his eyes. In their distraction they could not have said whether these were kisses or just words and looks. Their souls found themselves in each other, wedded together, and, in love with each other, rose above the earth like two spring clouds.

XI

One spring night a violent rainstorm seemed about to drown the world. Streams of rain hammered on the roof and spattered against the tightly closed shutters. The rooms were plunged in an impenetrable darkness. For hours Miss Salomea had been lying sleepless on her bed in the large drawing room. Odrowąż's door was partly closed, since she always closed it now when she went to bed.

All the unhappy thoughts that love had given rise to had extended over her that black and monstrous night. It seemed to her that they were circling like an accursed swarm around her bed and that their crooked fingers were plunging into her hair and raising her head from its sleep. What should she do? What action should she take? How could she reconcile her dilemma and come to terms with herself? With what could she calm her insistent heartache, stifle her sobs and the blind blows from the inner force of her pain?

A thousand times that night she summoned the courage for various courses of action. She would run away with him! She would perish with him somewhere in battle, in some savage, brutal, truly Muscovite encounter! She would die with him, here or elsewhere, so long as she was not left there without him!

How would that be possible? Not to know where he had gone or what had happened to him! A stranger had come and had become an all-powerful force governing her soul and filling her world. Now was she to wait for news and never receive any? To live without him when he was life itself? To remain in this place, remembering every moment, reliving everything that had happened, and to wait in vain, to wait for some terrible news! Every object would cease to be itself and instead would become an image or a memory. Or perhaps to learn that he had survived and was alive somewhere, but was with another woman, living in such and such a place . . . Through the gloom of night she saw an unknown face, the eyes of a woman gazing into his eyes, and she almost died from that vision, plunged into profound torment. How could she bear this suffering?

From time to time she jumped up from her bed, planning some act that would deliver him over to her. After all, he was still there! There, behind that door! She would call to him in a whisper and he would awaken. He would answer in his own quiet, sweet whisper. She could see him, touch him with her hands, talk to him, and listen to him. What joy! She reveled in her happiness, embracing it the way a mother embraces her child. She laid this passing moment on her burning heart and rocked it on her bosom, begging that it would be allowed to go on as long as possible, forever!

But her awareness of her happiness intensified even more and revealed the inexorable truth: that the moment was passing, that the day and the night would pass in their turn, and that the coming day might be the last. And again the impulse burst out: What should she do? How could she save the situation? How should she begin? What should she begin? What should she dare?

She thought of her father, and her heart stopped within her. She looked upon her love for him with an unblinking eye and weighed it against the exact measure of her new, ill-starred love. That force no one could comprehend, that nothing, became everything and swallowed up everything else into itself. She heard voices: *That's Mija for you! So that's what she came to!* Ordinary, everyday things, vulgar stories. *She slept with an insurgent who came to the house. No one was watching over her, so she took advantage of the situation.* A boundless, bottomless torment, the fearful power of love; then the strength of human judgment in these words. How cruel it was! This human frenzy! Flames licked at her head, and her heart seethed in fury. She sobbed into her pillow.

So what should she do? "Say nothing and forget," as older women always advised. She sat up abruptly, in wild despair; she knew she would never forget and that it was all too much for her. When the days that she saw in a distant haze finally arrived, she would suffocate in her agony. That must be what it meant to "say nothing and forget." How could she forget that face, those eyes, that smile, the sound of his voice! What force existed, what way existed, that would make her forget? She knew that there was no such force anywhere and that nothing in the world could draw it out of her. For how could she remove from her soul her whole world, how could she tear out everything that ruled that world?

Again she considered. The strangest, most improbable plans, the very thought of which a moment ago had sent shivers running down her spine, seemed natural and easy to carry out. But before the moment ended, the wall of reality rose up. The gates closed to the right and left, and the silent prison of life put chains on her hands.

What should she do about her father's love? Trample it into the ground, thrust it away? He would come in the night and find her gone. Szczepan would tell him what had happened. She hadn't been killed by the enemy, she hadn't been raped by the Russian troops—which, in the interests of a righteous cause, he could have borne with soldierly stoicism, leaving judgment in the hands of the Lord God. Instead she had given herself vilely to the insurgent. She had run away with him and was roaming the land with him somewhere. And in this way fatherly love, a profound, natural feeling as simple as breathing itself, appeared as something bad, as violence and tyranny.

How deep was her despair! How could she understand this within herself; what force could she use to overcome it and to punish it? She rushed to this fearful apparition to fight it and stamp it out; then, suddenly touched by a thought, she looked in another direction. Beautiful visions appeared before her. She traveled with him, with her husband, to distant, foreign, happy lands. No longer was there that abominable wickedness stalking the roads, the squares, and the houses of this downtrodden land by night, hammering at windows and disturbing one's sleep! No longer were there torments of humiliation and agonies of shame, the quaking of female nakedness before the eyes of foreign soldiers! She extended her hands into the darkness, toward the happiness that lay behind the partially closed door.

But her hands were seized and broken by fate as they reached out; she had to draw them back. As she sat on the bed with her head hung low, she sank her fingers into her loosened hair. And, just as her fingers played with her hair, so her thoughts took her problems strand by strand and examined them. A passing dreaminess, a blessed stilling of her emotions, and a lassitude of will bore her into a realm of semiconsciousness where improbable facts became reality. She saw foreign cities and sunny lands. People passed by speaking in an unknown tongue. Events occurred that her soul had never imagined, and issues arose that her mind had never before addressed. She saw the faces of people, the shapes of buildings, the colors of the fields, avenues, and copses of trees in that sunny, imagined country. It was there, far away, that her journey with her noble lord took place . . .

Suddenly, in the midst of this half-sleep, a distant thud sounded at the other end of the house, as if someone had fired a gun or dealt a strong blow to an empty vessel. There followed a silence that was all the more profound and complete. Her hair stood on end, and panic passed through her sleepy body. Her ear, alert and straining intently, imagined another thud. Was that a second boom or not? It must have been, for it made her body tremble like a leaf. Dominik! A moment later something blew through the room as if the door to the great drawing room had opened wide without a sound. Oh, Lord! He was standing there in the doorway! A black figure with a white face!

She covered her eyes with her hands, curled into a ball, and buried her face in her pillow, but she could not efface the image of the figure from her sight. She was racked by fear. Something rushed forward, bones rattling, ribs hurtling. She couldn't bear it! She jumped to her feet and gave a terrified scream.

From behind the door the duke called out once, then again. He asked in a whisper what was wrong. Were the soldiers hammering at the front door? The sound of the rain muffled his words, and the pattering of raindrops on the roof made it difficult to make out what he was saying. Miss Mija was so afraid that she did not know what was happening to her; her whole body shaking, she slipped out of bed and walked through the darkness in her nightgown, staring all the while at the door of the drawing room, where she could virtually see the figure of Dominik standing there. She gave another scream, and, no longer rational, she reached Odrowąż's door. She rushed into his room with a cry, burning with terror, her teeth chattering. It was only here, once she stood by his bed, that she came to her senses and realized what she had done. He saw her white figure in the darkness, reached out his hands, and found her clenched fists.

"What is it?" he asked.

"D-Dominik!" she stammered, unable to calm down.

"Where?"

"There, behind me!"

"No one's there!"

"He's standing in the doorway!"

"It's just an illusion."

"He already began throwing down the barrels."

"You're imagining things!"

"Didn't you hear it?"

"That's nonsense! The vats have dried out in that drafty room; now they've soaked up some of the moisture from the rain and they're making cracking noises as they expand."

"Best not talk like that! . . ."

He stroked her hands tenderly, trying to reassure her. Each stroke did in fact calm her, yet at the same time it also touched her with tongues of fire. She wanted to take her hands from his, but he would not let her. Instead he pulled them closer, to his lips, to his breast. He held them to his neck, to his forehead, and he touched his own face with them. She leaned forward imperceptibly, drawn by him, and felt his breath on her cheek. She was unable to move away, even to move her head. She felt a heavenly joy when his hands enfolded her through her nightgown and drew her unresisting into his bed.

Her ineffable rapture utterly defeated her reason, her memory, her consciousness, her awareness of the darkness, her sight, and her hearing. She alone took the place of everything else. She gave a sigh of insatiable pleasure as her entire body embraced the man she loved so much. She answered whisper with whisper, every kiss with a kiss, each caress with another. She became like a wave on the sea that is engulfed unknowingly by another wave; like an airy cloud that turns into another cloud; like a tree branch that rocks obediently in the wind, ignorant of where or wherefore.

All her thoughts were dissolved; her fear of parting ceased, and her terrible dilemmas found a simple solution. She began to talk about the thoughts that had been tormenting her as she tossed on her bed in the other room. When he asked why she hadn't come to him long before, since she was so afraid and so concerned, she had no answer. Indeed, she seemed foolish and cowardly to herself. She experienced this moment in her life as happiness that had no bounds, no measure, no beginning, and no end. This moment resolved everything. She laid her beautiful arms beneath her beloved's head, drew to herself this man who had been snatched from death, and cradled him cherishingly on her pure bosom just as, not long before, she had cherished the very moment of love-filled happiness in which she was able to live with him under the same roof.

Odrowąż felt her hard, firm body beneath his hands; he felt the maidenly beauty of her hips, her breasts, her arms, and her legs. He became deaf and blind, lost his reason, and went mad with rapture. He thought he was dying. His being was absorbed into her and no longer existed as a separate entity. He held her in his arms and was transformed into pure happiness. Their kisses became more and more insatiable, fiery, endless. Cries of delight escaped their lips. Tender words fell on mouths, on eyes, on breasts, on hair . . .

The rain beat down on the roof, lashed the walls, and echoed behind the closed shutters in the dark, impenetrable night.

XII

At long last, a Jewish two-horse wagonette pulled up in front of the veranda, and from its depths there emerged both Mr. and Mrs. Rudecki. Mr. Rudecki's wife had managed to have him released from prison on a hefty bail; but he was sick. He was able to get around with a walking stick, yet he looked poorly and did not speak. Mrs. Rudecka too had changed beyond recognition. They seemed to care little about the situation they found at their home.

A bed was made up for Mr. Rudecki in his old study, and he retired immediately. Mrs. Rudecka and Salomea inspected the rooms and the various nooks and crannies of the house. When she found a stranger in her ward's bedchamber, the mistress of the house expressed neither surprise nor disapproval. When she was told who he was and why he was staying there, she merely gave a nod of her head, deep in gloomy thought. Two of her sons had perished in the uprising. One had been so brutally hacked to pieces that she had been unable to recover his remains. The other she had found in a winding-sheet, with a tricolored cockade at his neck. She had watched as he and his comrades in arms had been taken and thrown without any casket into a common grave. A third son was still at large somewhere; no one knew if he was alive or dead, unharmed or wounded. And what of it that her sons had been dragged across snowy fields by wild horses and had had no roof over their heads, or even boards for a casket in this country for which they had given their lives, while a stranger had found care and comfort in their family home? Her heart was indifferent to it all. She sank into thought, nodded her head, and left the room.

At this time Odrowąż had had a relapse. One night about two weeks before the Rudeckis returned, Ryfka had knocked on the window to let them know that the Russian army was on its way.

Before there was time to wake the cook, the manor was surrounded and the duke had to slip out barefoot and in his nightshirt through the side hallway into the garden. He ran up the hill behind the outbuildings and hid in the bushes till the soldiers had gone away.

When they found him the following morning, he was freezing cold and barely conscious. He developed a high fever and came down with a sickness they could not identify, for there was no doctor to give it a name. For several days and nights he was delirious. It seemed as if he were about to die. When the Rudeckis came home he was already much better, but his condition still gave cause for concern. The fever persisted. The sick man ate and drank nothing and simply stared glassily ahead.

After a sleepless first night in his room, in the morning Mr. Rudecki rose early and, despite his wife's protestations, put on his thick boots and the clothes he used to wear and left the house. He stepped off the veranda and inspected everything: the dismantled fences, the garden overgrown with weeds, the earth around the manor trampled by horses' hooves, the burned outbuildings standing like blackened posts amid the greenery . . . He stepped into the empty stables, the empty cattle sheds, the empty potato clamps. He gazed at the unplowed and unsown fields and at the whole emptiness that had settled on the area.

He stood in the courtyard, looking intently all around. Then he returned to the house. But once he was inside, he had a sudden attack. He was carried to his bed in a sorry state. Mrs. Rudecka instructed Szczepan at any cost to hire a pair of horses from the village or from the Jews and to bring from the small town nearby the healer, who was known throughout the region where he practiced.

In the evening the healer, an elderly Orthodox Jew, arrived at Niezdoły. He looked the owner of the manor over, ascertained his condition, and smacked his lips. He recommended peace and quiet and prescribed a variety of remedial measures. At Miss Salomea's pressing request, he also examined the insurgent, in great fear and even greater secrecy. He found a serious, dangerous illness. He refused to name it. He forbade anyone to talk with the duke or even to have close contact with him; and he warned them not to move him, saying openly that any attempt to do so could kill him. Finally, rolling his eyes in a wise and mysterious fashion, he announced that the Lord God willing, both sick men might yet recover. He himself could do little. With that he left.

Mr. Rudecki did not survive the sights that had awaited him in Niezdoły. Three days later he passed away. He was given a simple, modest funeral, in keeping with the times and the circumstances. There was no crowd from the village. Only a few of the older villagers called by the manor to see the master, as if out of curiosity, to check whether he really was dead. The casket was made by a local craftsman whose usual job was to provide his neighbors in the village with their last shelter.

After Mr. Rudecki's body had been taken to the parish cemetery and buried, sadder times yet fell upon Niezdoły Manor. The widow and solitary mother shed tears by night. Now everything was tangled together: an aversion to life and the need to continue that life for her remaining children; a repugnance for any kind of action and the necessity to act providently. There was another wave of searches by the Russian soldiers and overnight stays by isolated groups of insurgents from the Polish forces.

In addition to all this, in the forlorn desert of mourning there came and went the eternal illusion of the wanderings of Dominik's shade, who seemed to scoff at it all. The widow continued to hear his footsteps, the slamming of doors, his laughter in that distant, empty room behind a dozen closed doors . . . It seemed to her that he was forever snickering with glee that everything had gone wrong for the family, for that house, for their happiness. His torment, his world-weariness, and his savage death had taken their revenge. So he walked at night about the empty manor, passing by the furniture, peeping through cracks in doors, lurking behind wardrobes . . . He looked upon it all and chuckled till he was fit to burst, the evil spirit of Niezdoły Manor.

XIII

The lovely month of May arrived, and Józef Odrowąż still had not recovered his health. The green of springtime covered the wounds of the lacerated earth. Its injuries were concealed by feathers, leaves, stems, curly stalks, and multifarious shades of color that were a pleasure for the eye to behold. In the same way that they absorbed moisture and decay, with their colors, their forms, and the unending power of their growth, they tried to soak up the sufferings of souls and to destroy the memory of what had fallen and died. Everything grew and flourished in the interests of new life and to the detriment of death. At night a nightingale sang by the water, near the hill at the foot of which Hubert Olbromski had found his resting place.

In Niezdoły Manor a different kind of life began. Mrs. Rudecka began taking on servants and farmhands, buying livestock, and establishing order, hard work, and discipline in the household. She had already begun to think about rebuilding the barns, the cattle sheds, and the granary. Dinners and suppers were cooked. Szczepan once again stood at his frying pans, saucepans, and kettles. He had at his disposition a scullery maid, a dirty young girl whose job it was to scrub the pots and pluck the chickens. He shouted at her with the utmost severity and pushed her around, repaying twice over his former powerlessness in the kitchen. Out of ancient habit he continued to talk to the fire, declaring, explaining, arguing, asserting, and refuting. At times the fire obviously disagreed with him vehemently, for the old man would stamp his worn-out shoes and shake his fist at it.

The whole time they were waiting for Miss Salomea's father, Mr. Brynicki, to come back. For many years now he had been the real head of the household and manager of the whole estate; they expected him to slip back home from the rebel army, take control, reintroduce order in the manor, repair the great old clock of the property and set it in motion once again. They waited in vain . . . One evening at suppertime a footsore countryman from far away in the Świętokrzyskie woods came to the manor and brought terrible news: Miss Salomea's father was dead.

He had been wounded in battle somewhere in the hills, and, seriously sick, he had gone into hiding in the cottages of country folk, good people who lived in a village in the woods near the monastery of St. Catherine. He had treated himself as best he knew how, using time-honored soldier's methods. He applied various ointments to his wounds, drank an infusion of special herbs that he knew about. All in vain! The moment came when he realized his life was coming to an end.

He asked the villager who had taken him in and hidden him to bear news to his daughter. Taking a rough, stiff scrap of dull-colored paper that he had acquired at some point on his marches and, for lack of a writing implement, using his penknife to sharpen the last lead bullet that was left in his bag, he had written his daughter a message from his deathbed.

He commended her to God and to the kindness of her relatives, with whom he had broken bread for so many years and whose troubles he had shared. He entreated her to protect her good name and to live and work honestly. About himself he reported that he was seriously wounded and that it was not possible for him to leave the place where he was writing or to be treated elsewhere. He was too weak to walk. His head rang. He could not see clearly. He wrote too that in his soul he no longer felt his former strength and that great sorrow was in his heart. In a postscript he added that he was sending his dear daughter, Salomea, the last few pennies he owned: forty-seven Polish zlotys. Once more commending his "little daughter Mija" to God, who was in his heart as he was dying and who "watches unchangingly over the world," he bade her farewell and blessed her.

The countryman who had brought the letter added from himself that the elderly insurgent had died shortly after writing the message and that the villagers had buried him secretly at night in the cemetery of the village chapel there in the Świętokrzyski region. The man untied a bundle and conscientiously laid out on the bench the forty-seven zlotys that had been entrusted to him. He then recounted a number of details of the insurgent's last moments.

This man was entirely different from the villagers of Niezdoły. He supported the "cause," like all his neighbors in those parts. This journey to bring news was the first time he had traveled to the outside world; on his way, he had been deeply surprised by the country folk he had encountered who railed against the "Poles." For in his region people believed in their own and looked to the Polish side; they helped the insurgents in their marches, took in the wounded and concealed them, and the younger, more fiery spirited among them even joined the rebel army.

He was offered thanks and given a meal, and then he set off back home: he needed as quickly as possible to begin his long journey, which lay along little-known, rarely frequented trails, through the woods, so as not to run into the Russian army. Miss Salomea accompanied him for a couple of miles along the edges of the fields, that last witness and dismal bringer of news. After they parted, for a long, long while she watched him, the messenger who had come to her from her father and was now returning to the place where he lay. The man's figure grew smaller; it became like the earth, like the twilight . . .

When he was so far away that he disappeared from sight, she sank into profound despair. The news had brought death to her soul. Her torment was twice, thrice, a thousandfold the greater when she compared dates and realized that her father had been on his lonely deathbed exactly at the time she had given herself to her lover. He had been dying right then, or at about the time of that unforgettable night when it had seemed to her that her father's love was a burden and a constraint. Deadened, with no tears in her eyes, she ran back through the blooming fields to the house. A cry of anguish burst from her lips. Then, suddenly, she burned with an even greater, more terrible, singular, and boundless love for her adored one.

XIV

Mrs. Rudecka decided to act in the name of the whole family. She set to work on the household. Yet everything now came out wrong, went to waste, and got broken. Relations had undergone an irreversible change. People were different: the lower they had previously bowed their heads, the more they were now impudent and hostile. Everything disappeared, stolen almost before their eyes. All their efforts crumbled and were absorbed into nothingness.

Miss Brynicka was the younger and healthier of the two women, and she had to take on the lion's share of the work. So now too she did not sleep enough and hardly ate at all. Her concern for the duke reached the point of permanent desperation, forever hidden by a cheerful expression, jokes, and good humor to ward off suspicion. Her sleep turned into a half-waking, half-dreaming state known only to women in love. One ear was in the netherworld of daydreams, the other listened intently to his breathing, sensitive to every murmur. Her thoughts broke loose, rose, and soared a hundred miles up in the air, yet at the same time there was no break in her constant vigilance, her prognoses and logical inferences regarding the development and current state of his illness.

The soldiers were not marching through or intruding so often now, as the insurgents were holed up in the woods and so drew the enemy away from human settlements. Moreover, the rebels' main area of operations had temporarily moved elsewhere.

Both the women of the old manor took full advantage of these circumstances and worked from dawn till dusk. There was so much catching up to do! They laughed aloud and spoke only of cheerful matters, in order to conceal their true, inner feelings—and perhaps also to use the laughter to exert pressure on their souls and to cure their hearts of the habit of crying.

Yet they were not always successful. One sunny day in the garden they were airing out some chests that had been closed up all winter. The two relatives took things out of the chests and hung them out in the garden. They worked briskly, and their labors put them in a good mood. But at one point Mrs. Rudecka went into the house and for a long time did not return.

Then the younger woman heard a convulsive cry at the other end of the house. She ran in and searched room after room. In the corner of the dining room—the large room by the kitchen—she found Mrs. Rudecka sitting on the floor next to a wardrobe. In a drawer the wretched mother had found children's clothes belonging to Gucio, the son who had been hacked to death in the uprising. She had seized in her crossed arms what used to be his little jacket with gold buttons, hugged it to her chest, and, squatting on the ground, she was rocking to and fro, blind, deaf, and senseless with pain. Savage cries like the call of the kite came from her compressed lips. She was helped up from the floor; she opened her eyes, came to herself, apologized for her unseemly behavior, and went back to work.

Any news from the outside world, any rattle of wheels in the courtyard, caused trembling, panic, and the torment of flight. In Niezdoły Manor, they came to hate the sound of wheels and the clatter of horses' hooves. Then, one afternoon in the second half of May, a large, shining carriage drawn by four tired but well-fed horses pulled up in front of the veranda. Mrs. Rudecka ran into the hallway in consternation and peered out through a side window, anticipating some new calamity. Miss Salomea also stared at the carriage from her hiding place behind the net curtains in the great drawing room.

Fortunately it was a woman who emerged from the carriage, not a man, which in itself was something of a relief. The visitor was tall, and despite her graying hair, her face bore signs of beauty. She lifted the veil on her black hat and looked all about her, clearly expecting someone to come out and receive her. But in those times homes were inhospitable and people did not wish to see other people. The mistress did not hurry to welcome the lady, in the hope that, as she had come, so she would leave at once in her gleaming carriage.

The lady in black walked up to the veranda and began to climb the steps. There were only a few steps, yet it seemed that she would not be able to make it to the top. They had to open the door and go out to meet her. When Mrs. Rudecka appeared on the threshold, the visitor noticed her and nodded several times. She was as white as a sheet, with rings under her eyes and discoloring around her mouth. Standing on the first step, she stumbled against the second, and with a curious awkwardness she knelt on it. In a tremulous voice, through teeth that chattered as though she had a fever, she asked:

"This is the manor of the Niezdoły estate, is it not?"

"Yes," replied the mistress.

"Might you be Mrs. Rudecka?"

"I am. . ."

"I have been told . . . I was informed that in the winter a wounded man was being looked after here . . . I've been searching for three months. I was told . . . He's a tall, slim young lad with brown hair."

"What is his name?"

"His family name is Odrowąż, his Christian name Józef."

"Are you perhaps his mother?"

"That's right . . ."

"Please come in."

"Is he here?"

"Yes."

"Is he alive?"

"He is."

"Oh, my Lord! Here in this house?"

"Right here. Please come inside."

But the visitor no longer had the strength to enter. The smile of happiness that had appeared on her lips and on her face seemed to represent the last limits of her energy, all that was left of any strength she had. She slipped to her knees, and reaching out her hands to Mrs. Rudecka, she fainted. Miss Salomea ran to her assistance, helped the duke's mother up, and brought her round with water. The driver of the carriage, who had heard the conversation, lashed the horses vigorously, turned the foursome about in the courtyard, and quickly drove off. Duchess Odrowąż was carried in by the two women of Niezdoły to the room on the right, at a distance from the wounded man's bedroom. She had barely come round when she looked at Miss Salomea and asked:

"Was it you who saved my boy's life?"

"Who told you that?"

"The doctor," she whispered.

"Dr. Kulewski?"

"Yes. I looked everywhere; I visited all the battlefields, every inn, manor, and village; I asked everyone. Finally . . ."

"But he's seriously ill . . ."

"Ill! What's wrong with him?"

"I don't know. He was wounded."

"I know about the wounds. On his head, on his back . . . his eye . . . The doctor told me everything. Is that bullet still in the wound?"

"The bullet is out."

"It's out!"

"But he's come down with some kind of sickness."

"My Lord! Where is he?"

"You won't be able to see him now, because he might not survive the shock."

"He's that ill?"

"That was what the healer said when he examined him."

"We'll fetch a doctor!" exclaimed the mother.

"Very well!" whispered the younger woman just as quietly as before.

They leaned together and began whispering to each other, as if in the presence of an eavesdropping enemy, about the details of the sickness, its subtlest signs and symptoms, conjecturing about ways to treat it. They forgot about the outside world, immediately connected by shared feelings that from the very beginning had manifested themselves in both women and had bound them together and united them. Duchess Odrowąż sat in the corner of the sofa with Salomea at her side on a stool. With an inconspicuous gesture, the mother embraced this unknown girl, brought her hands round her neck, drew her to herself, held her arms, her head, and her back, and together with her began to rock in a transport of gratitude. She passed her delicate fingers over the young woman's shining hair and a hundred times over stroked her cheeks with her hands. Unaware of what she was doing, in the madness of her delight she took Miss Mija's hands and brought them to her lips so suddenly that the latter barely had time to pull them away with a cry.

Opposite them Mrs. Rudecka sat in her armchair. She wore a courteous smile and was urbane and calm, as was proper in the presence of a guest. With her head inclined curiously, she listened to the conversation and shared the joy of a mother who had found her son on the long, confusing, twisted pathways of the Polish uprising. Yet if the truth be told, her eyes did not see the other two women, and her ears were not entirely attending to the details they discussed endlessly. Her eyes looked through the two of them at the windowpanes or the rough walls of the house, at the fields, the distant wooded valleys, and perhaps boldly into the terrible, inaccessible eyes of God himself.

The duchess had forgotten about the outside world, about social customs and all the formalities that needed to be observed first; she asked Miss Salomea to be allowed to see her son. But the young nurse would not agree. She knew the sick man's condition well; she was aware that at the sight of his mother his fever would worsen a hundredfold and that such a fever could kill him. They negotiated for a long time. The one continued to implore, the other would not yield. In the end, they agreed that the mother would see her only child through the crack in the door.

Forgetting about Mrs. Rudecka, they tiptoed through the entrance hall and into the drawing room. Miss Salomea passed through this room and entered the bedroom, leaving the door ajar behind her. Through the gap it was possible to see the sick man's face. Lady Odrowąż put her eyes to this gap so quietly that Salomea didn't know whether she was already in place or whether she was still standing in the middle of the drawing room.

In the meantime, the insurgent's mother, creeping up as softly as possible to the opening between the door and the jamb, slipped to her knees and looked. With a prayer on her trembling lips, and through endless streams of tears, she gazed upon the face so dear to her. In this way an hour passed, then another. Miss Salomea could not make her stand from her place or move away. It was only when evening drew on and began to hide the sick man that the duchess was pulled away by force to one of the rooms at the other end of the house, where a bed had been made up for her.

XV

Life in the manor changed. The duchess brought in doctors to save her son, compensating them generously for their advice and their pains. Under a variety of pretexts, she hired servants to cater to his needs. She paid for everything, laying down money left and right, caring about nothing except that her beloved only child should regain his health.

Among others, the old cook, Szczepan Podkurek, made money and advanced in life owing to these circumstances. When Miss Salomea recounted the many times that the old man had saved the young insurgent's life, how he had given him his old shoes and had fed him with kasha, and how much he had done for him thereafter, Lady Odrowąż scarcely knew how to thank him. What could she do for him beyond giving him money? So she handed him a purse filled with gold coins, first offering him a thousand thanks.

The old man stuffed the purse in his inside pocket and guarded it with his life. The possession of such a large amount of gold turned his thoughts quite upside down. As before, he continued to wear a coarse shirt, dirty, tattered trousers with holes in the knees, and old boots with wooden soles. As before, his head was never covered, for it was a long time since he had owned a hat or a cap. He continued to cook for the mistresses and the servants; he had to prepare everything himself according to the wishes of the lady visitor, who asked for ever more fanciful dishes for the sick young gentleman.

The possession of money, then, was something internal and unreal. Time and again he would thrust his hand into his pocket and pat his treasure, checking to see whether his senses were not deceiving him and to confirm that he, Szczepan the cook, really was the rich man he kept dreaming about. When no one else was about in the kitchen, in his old way he would talk with the fire. The conversation was invariably about theft:

"He stole it!" he would rage at the flames, shaking his fists. "Who did he steal it from? Out with it, since you know who! He stole it! It just goes to show . . . He stole a purse like that—and who from? Did someone bring it here? Were they carrying it around, did they leave it somewhere, or what? People are swine! The lady gave me it, Her Grace, for saving her son's life. That was what she gave it me for! She even stroked my mug with her little hand and gave me a smacker on the forehead. I tell you, swine, not people! Turns out there's no witness to these shenanigans . . . Oh, sure! Am I the one at fault? Did I know what she would do to me when she wandered into the kitchen? If I'd known, I would've called you in, you bastards: Come and get a load of this! You could've just stood in the corner and watched. You'd have seen how it was for yourselves, damn you! She stood here, by the fireplace; I looked at her, she looked at me. Then she went and took this purse, she took it out of her bag and put it in my hand . . . Here you are, my friend, she says—those were the duchess's words—God grant you thanks! You can buy whatever you wish with it. So what am I supposed to do now? Eh? You tell me, you swine! If I have to swear an oath, I will! And she'll back me up that that's how it was. She was standing here by the fireplace . . . I looked at her, she looked at me. Then she went and took this purse, she took it out of her bag and put it in my hand . . . He stole it! He didn't steal it, you bastard, it's mine . . ."

The fire clearly did not believe this story; doubt and suspicious laughter crackled away in it, for Szczepan shouted and heaped upon it a series of vulgar obscenities that cannot be repeated here.

Every so often, when he had a free moment, he would slip away up the hill behind the garden, and there, concealing himself in the densest thicket, he would take the purse from his inside pocket. With great care, one after another he would pull out the golden coins, lay them in a row on the spreading leaves, and try to count them.

But the exact measurement of the amount surpassed his arithmetical abilities. He was unable to evaluate precisely the extent of his fortune. He kept recalling something from years ago about large figures and complex equations involving many tens. His thoughts were immersed in the mysterious darkness of human calculation; he reflected and extracted from the nothingness some personal system of his own for adding certain coins to certain others in order to establish their sum; he added laboriously, like farmhands tossing bundles of hay on pitchforks into the barn.

At certain points he got mixed up and went wrong, since it all turned on the unknown value of the gold coins. He had to be content with lying on his belly, staring at the glittering disks spread out on the green leaves, and baring the gap in his front teeth at them in a smile of indescribable happiness. He did not dare ask anyone to confirm the amount of his property, for fear of betrayal, deceit, theft, or banditry. So he left things as they were.

After a while the desire arose in him to return to his "country," in other words, to his own village, which was situated about fifteen miles from his kitchen and which he had not visited for over twenty years, busy with his cooking at the manor. He imagined the journey to those distant parts and his triumphal entry into his native village with his treasure at his bosom. Through a haze he once again saw the village: the mud, the roads, the cottages, the tumbledown wattle fences, the ragged, stooping trees; once again he heard the dogs barking, people squabbling, and the creaking of the well sweep at the point where the pond by the highway was deepest. He laughed aloud as he stared into the fire and told it what a spectacle there would be when he returned home with a great fortune in his pocket.

"I'll turn to the right by the shrine, through that hole in Walek's fence, and I'll go down the path to the stile by Bartoś's barn. The dogs know me there—though, come to think of it, they may not be alive anymore. Ha, ha, Bartoś's wife herself'll try to trip me up . . . 'Sit down, Szczepan; you've traveled many a mile, of that I'm sure.' 'And I suppose you don't know yourself why you're talking like that? I know you and Bartoś only too well!' . . ."

Yet the old man's plans for his journey evidently kept going awry, because he was always angry and storming, stamping his feet at someone and shaking his fist. The choice of a time to go caused him real difficulties, for when he thought about that moment, the mountains of work that he had to do made it disappear without a trace, so he could not seize it. He even made up a little song, which he croaked out as he snickered at the fire under the range. The song was a short one. It began with the words:

> It's not that I'm running away, I'm just leaving,
> For the pain I've felt here has my heart all a-grieving . . .

But despite that grief, and despite the alluring visions of his home village, Szczepan bustled about the fireplace in Niezdoły in the same clothes and with the same assiduity. He had no hope of carrying out the plan referred to in his song. In fact, there was no possibility of it even, for there was ever more work of ever more different kinds. He had to make the sick man fortifying chicken broth and various elaborate dishes. The duchess herself stood by the grimy chimney, boiling or frying meals for her son. How could Szczepan leave her alone, without a cook? Who would make the meals for his own mistress and also for Miss "Bawlomea," whose guardian he had effectively become after old Mr. Brynicki's death?

Duchess Odrowąż was still not allowed to show herself to her son. She watched him secretly through the crack in the door. Salomea, playing the role of a sister of mercy with him, gradually prepared the sick man for a meeting with his mother. She took advantage of every moment of improvement in his health to talk of her or to suggest that he might like to write to her. Then she asked if she could send word in his name and request her to come. To begin with the sick man protested and would not agree. Later he gave up and began to speak of his mother himself. Finally, fooled by the story about the letters, he began to inquire whether there hadn't been any reply. Salomea made up a whole series of stories about how the letter had been delivered, how his mother was already on her way, and how she would probably be arriving soon . . .

Duchess Odrowąż listened to their conversations at the door, trembling to be able at last to draw close to her son. From afar she captured every look of his, every gesture, every breath, and every moan; her lungs shared his cough and her heart the quickened pounding of his heart.

Watching everything in this way, she could not fail to see the truth about the sick man's feelings for his nurse and his relationship with her. The expression in her son's eyes whenever the young woman entered or left the room told her everything within the first few days of that curious coexistence. At this point the wretched mother wished for only one thing: to save her child's life. How much agony she suffered at every rustle, every rumble or clatter of hooves that signaled the arrival of the army! She was as obedient as a child with Salomea, for the latter knew what to do when things went wrong and how to save the situation. The poor mother learned in a twinkling all the ways—the spying, the hiding places, and the escape routes—and in a twinkling did what she had to. In emergencies the gloomy, dirty Szczepan took charge of her, issuing orders that were peremptory and brooked no objections. She was as compliant as a serving woman. She ran where she was told to, without a murmur performing all the things that previously Szczepan had alone been responsible for.

In those few days Salomea and Józef Odrowąż's mother grew so close together that they became as one person. They communicated with each other by thoughts; above all, the feelings of each were an open book for the other. What for anyone else was only a word, a name, was for them the entire world. One understood the other's emotions, could recognize them when they were merely referred to, could see them for what they were, and could move about them as if they were a land in another world, filled with hills, flower-covered valleys, cliffs, and deathly ravines. While the injured man slept, they sat in each other's arms and recounted their impressions and their memories. A thousand times over Salomea divulged all the vicissitudes of the young man's stay at the manor, all the stages of his sufferings, the mishaps, sorrows, and joys. For the mother it was all so fascinating and perpetually of interest that Salomea had to repeat it over and again.

They were incapable of talking about anything else. Their world existed only in the room where the young man lay. The more his life hung by a thread, the deeper, more ecstatic, and the closer to madness these two women's love for each other became. With a single squeeze of the hand they conveyed more than could be expressed in a long conversation. With one look they told each other everything. When the sick man coughed or groaned, they ran like two wings of the same angel to tend to him, to mop his brow, and to comfort him—one openly, the other in secret, one with words and a tender touch, the other only with a look, a hand stretched out toward him, and a prayer.

XVI

The fever abated. The sickness had reached a peak and had begun to recede. Through the open window the smell of trees in blossom and the scent of nighttime flowers wafted in from the garden. The warm wind had a salubrious effect on the sick man. It seemed that the moonlight creeping into the room healed his young organism with its rays and that the morning sun brought him vigor more effectively than milk. He began to sit on the edge of the bed; his appetite returned and, along with it, his physical strength.

At this time his mother entered his room. Her presence had a dramatic effect on the convalescent. It turned out that there had been truth in the warning given by the experienced healer from the town. For a long time the young duke could not come to as he lay in his mother's arms. Yet once he overcame his shock, his recovery progressed even more quickly.

There also appeared the greatest worry of all: that at this very moment there should be a search by the army and all should come to naught. By now many people knew of the insurgent's presence at the manor. More and more servants had been hired, and it had become impossible to conceal the fact from them. The entire village knew perfectly well what was going on. The reopening of the farm had brought various people to the manor, any one of whom, not even out of evil intent or the desire for ill-gotten gains, but through simple gossip, could have betrayed the wounded man's presence at any moment and risked his undoing. There was no longer anywhere to conceal him in an emergency, since the hay had been removed from the partition in the barn, and it was difficult to come up with new hiding places.

Duchess Odrowąż was fully aware that she was exposing this

wretched household and its mistress, who had already borne so many blows, to further perils—that she was poisoning her days and nights with the matter of her son. Everything pointed to a decision to take him away. Yet where could she take him in this country? The same danger lurked everywhere. She decided, then, that as soon as he could stand on his feet, at any cost she would escape across the border with him.* Her resolution was additionally prompted by the terrible worry that the moment he was even a little better, he would tear himself from her arms to rejoin the rebel army—that, and one other consideration . . .

The duchess had long seen her son's relationship with Mrs. Rudecka's ward. In her maternal heart she felt a million things for the girl: she loved her; she worshiped her for her devotion to Józef; with her alone she shared the deepest emotions of her soul. Yet she shuddered whenever she thought of her son taking such a person as his wife . . . Duke Odrowąż simply could not marry Miss Brynicka. Despite all the love she bore her, the duchess was naturally unable to overcome her aversion for certain of the young lady's views, parochial notions, and habits and expressions she had taken from the manor.

She bit her lip agitatedly when she saw the expressions on both their faces, for she knew that this was no ordinary case of flirtation between a patient and his nurse, but a profound love. She could not sleep at night, agonizing over how to solve her problem. She was incapable of harming a girl like this, whose heart she held in her hand, for she alone had risen to the same zenith of love for her son as the duchess herself. She did not dare to meddle with her feelings or to hurt them. In her heart of hearts, she could not even disap-

*During the partition of Poland, the Austrian border was no more than twenty or thirty miles from the region where the novel takes place.—TRANS.

prove of their mutual love, the depths of which her mother's heart had plumbed.

She was caught on the horns of a dilemma. She possessed within her a thousand ways to resolve the issue and was unable to choose any one of them. Of one thing she was sure: She must rid her son of these feelings and must seize him, by force if necessary, and take him away from there. She longed only for one thing: to be across the border with him. Once she was there, she would arrange everything cleverly, reasonably, and properly. If only she could be there already! In the meantime, she lived amid danger, anxiety, and heartbreak.

She consulted with Mrs. Rudecka, and the latter of course agreed with her on every point. There remained the business of informing Salomea and her son. Yet at this juncture the mother's strength abandoned her. She had before her a task that was straightforward yet required the circumspection and intelligence of the most masterful diplomat—and perhaps the strength of the executioner's arm. Duchess Odrowąż wept hot, bitter tears as she observed Salomea and her troubles, her unreasoning and unthinking exertions and efforts for the wounded man, and her oblivious, crazy love, which she herself thought to be carefully concealed and yet which was in fact as plain as could be. Oh, how could she address those feelings with the implacable tone that was called for?. . . The duchess did not have the strength. She was also afraid of her son. She could not tell what he would say. She had already lived through one secret flight to the woods to join the insurgents.

In the meantime, amid these vacillations, which took place in the world—or rather the dreamy netherworld of the feelings—physical health as ever played its own part. When the young Odrowąż began to recover, his mother, who had not seen all the other stages of his illness, forgot about them and about everything else that had been associated with that illness. The sufferings, difficulties, and anxieties that had been borne, and the maneuvers and dodges that had been performed in order to bring her son back to health, shrank, grew distant, and disappeared. The sorrowful circumstances that had accompanied the story were lost in oblivion and were absorbed into nothingness; and along with this process, Miss Mija's contribution was also diminished. A new mountain of concerns about the future rose before the mother. And at present Salomea stood before that future as the chief obstacle. The mother's heart was now battling with her for the good of her son. And the thorn of antipathy had lodged in that heart . . .

Without telling anyone, Lady Odrowąż sent a generously paid messenger—she had found willing volunteers for the assignment in the inn at the crossroads—to the house of some aristocrats who lived not too far away, with a request for assistance. She received the promise of a carriage and horses, which would be provided immediately at a given sign to take her son over the border on the chosen day. The same individuals used their extensive contacts to arrange passports for foreign travel for her and her son, under assumed names. One day a hot, tired messenger brought her the passports. Józef Odrowąż's health was already good enough for them to undertake the journey, though he was still confined to bed. It was now time to set about resolving the matter once and for all.

One June evening, when the last arrangements had been made, and the carriage and horses sent for, the duchess took Salomea out into the garden and walked with her to the old arbor down by the river. The great trees rustled about them, covered with young leaves. The grapevine that twined about the columns and the broken roof of the arbor blocked out the dusk outside and made the interior darker still. The moment she crossed the threshold of the arbor, the duchess dropped down on a bench and drew Salomea to her. She seized her in an embrace and gave her a tender kiss. She held her to her heart and uttered dry sobs. Words stuck in her throat and could not prize open her clenched teeth. Tears began to pour from the duchess's eyes so profusely that they made the girl's face wet, filled the corners of her mouth with salt, moistened her neck, and even dripped onto her bosom beneath her loosened bodice.

Salomea's whole body trembled. Thoughts flared in the darkness of her emotions like the flashes on a summer's night that herald the approach of a storm. The tears that fell on her in some inexplicable way became the tracks of misery slowly trickling down to her heart, seeking it within her breast. The duchess's hands ever more powerfully and convulsively closed round Salomea's shoulders and neck, and her quiet, hollow voice said:

"Child! You love him . . ."

Salomea was silent, but the way her body shuddered provided an exact response.

"And he loves you. Is that right?"

Once again silence sufficed for a reply.

"And he's told you that he loves you?"

"He has."

"And you've told him, too?"

"Yes."

"Answer me right away now! Tell me the whole truth, without concealing anything! Will you tell me the truth?"

"I will."

Salomea felt a need to obey and a compulsion to confess the whole truth and nothing but. It was as if she had been stripped of her dresses, her underclothes, and her body, so that her powerless, trembling soul stood alone before her dark mistress.

"Have you kissed?"

"Yes."

"There in his room, at night?"

"Yes."

"Did you give yourself to him?"

"Yes."

"How many times?"

"I don't remember."

"Did he promise that he would marry you?"

"He did."

"And that was why you gave yourself to him?"

"No."

"Tell me now! Only the complete truth! . . . Will you answer me?"

"Yes."

"Swear to me now! May Dominik come and stand over your bed every night if you utter one word that's not true!"

"Oh!"

Salomea dropped onto the other woman's shoulder with a groan.

"Speak the truth, then! Have you ever been with anyone else the way you were with him?"

"No!"

"Not ever, not with anyone?"

"Never!"

"And no one ever kissed you before?"

"Well, yes, I've been kissed before . . ."

"By whom?"

"Someone here . . ."

"Who was it?"

"A cousin of mine."

"Did you love him?"

"No."

"Then why did you let him kiss you?"

"Because I rather liked him."

This confession seemed to give the duchess strength. Her voice became firmer; and the indomitable, conquering force of clear reason broke through in that voice.

"Listen, my child! Do you want Józef to rejoin the rebel army?"

"Oh, no!"

"Do you want him to be wounded again?"

"No!"

"Do you want him to get better?"

"Of course I do!"

"Then what should be done, what arrangements should be made so he can get better?"

"I don't know."

"Think with all your head, use your whole heart!"

"I can't think of anything."

"And what would you want, just for yourself?"

"To be with him, to serve him . . ."

"Exactly! Listen now . . . shouldn't we do this? If not, then suggest something else. I'll do whatever you wish."

"I can't think of anything. I'll be the one who follows your wishes."

"Then listen! I think that it's essential to take him away from here."

"Take him away . . ."

"Was that not what you thought?"

"I don't know."

"Where can he be taken in this country? I'll go somewhere, and they'll find him there! If I go somewhere else, they'll find him wherever he is! They'll put him in prison! They'll hang him before my eyes! Or in secret from me! What then? He must be taken abroad."

"Oh, my Lord!"

"But he won't go of his own accord. He'll have to be promised that as soon as his health improves, he'll be able to return to his unit. You have to help me to persuade him to go."

"*I* have to! . . ."

"He's not going to recover in these conditions. Tell me what you're thinking!"

"He did recover in these conditions."

"But can he stay here much longer? Will he himself want to stay once he's better?"

"No."

"Abroad, I'll soon have him on his feet again. And when he's well, to stop him going back to the rebels, I'll take him away to Italy."

"Italy!"

"It's only there that he can fully regain his health. And after all, that's what you want, too: that he should no longer go to war and be wounded all over again. Is that not the truth?"

"Yes."

"And if I'm wrong, if I'm not saying the truth, then you tell me what else to do. Your hard voice is of no use to me here."

Salomea's old dream of traveling with her husband in the distant, unknown land of Italy passed through her soul like a bloody torment. She recalled the cities she had imagined, the images of mountains and seas that her eyes had never beheld. She rallied herself before this terrible mistress of her fate and asked:

"And so there's no other way than for him to leave the country now, then later to travel to Italy?"

"None."

Józef's mother's voice was powerful, harsh, and piercing like a bullet. Salomea was silent. Cold assailed her shoulders and reached her innards. A prickly feeling of despair passed through her hair. An inner voice sounded through her mouth:

"What about me?"

Duchess Odrowąż spoke ever more quietly and distinctly, holding her to her side:

"You're still so young . . . You love him. You saved his life. He loves you. You've been together. I know everything, and I forgive you. But he's terribly ill now! Think about it, you, the only one who loves him . . . He has to be able to recuperate in peace and quiet, in a healthy climate, far away from these terrible fields and woods. He has to look at it all through different eyes. In his soul he has to curse these reckless enterprises, these foolish plans!"

In her profound anguish, Salomea suddenly saw the shade of her father—and also that of the man who lay buried in the earth close to the arbor. A proud resentment stirred within her. An unbreakable honor, which she had never before felt within herself, made her say:

"He will not curse these foolish plans!"

"But he must! That which deserves to be cursed must be cursed!"

"No! What they have done doesn't deserve to be cursed."

"My son must remember now that he has no business wasting away in squalid camps and hiding in the hay; that he is a gentleman, and was born a duke!"

Salomea heard the final note in her mistress's speech, and she understood it. Something closed up within her, like a lock to which no one would ever find the key. She said nothing. The trembling had ceased; all that was left in her being was the monotonous pain in her heart. She listened on as the duchess said:

"You're a second child to me . . . my only daughter! I shall never, ever forget you. On my deathbed I shall remember your face and your name. He too—believe me, my darling! He will remember you as his dearest one. And as for me, I shall never say a word against you to him. May God punish me if I'm not telling the truth! But you have a duty. Mrs. Rudecka brought you up; she was a mother to you when you were orphaned. Wasn't it so? Was she not a mother and a protectress to you?"

"Yes."

"And now it's she who is the orphan, the most wretched of people, the mother of murdered sons in that empty house. Would you have the heart to leave her alone, when the manor and the whole household rests upon your shoulders?"

Salomea gathered her courage and asked in the madness of her despair:

"Could I not be of use in some way on the journey to Italy?"

"In what character? As what?"

"As a servant."

"No, my child, you cannot be a servant. I would not agree to see you abased so. Precisely because we are not social equals I will not allow you to be abased. You could accompany Józef only as his wife . . . But of course that is impossible. You know full well yourself that it's impossible."

"Then what am I supposed to do?"

"Turn for help to God, to Józef's love for you, and that of the guardian who brought you up. Perhaps even to my love, if I shall find that favor in your heart. Enjoin your heart to silence . . . Time will heal the wound I'm inflicting on you at this moment. My little daughter, my dear little daughter. My dearest! My dearest! . . ."

The duchess slipped to her knees and, weeping, put her arms around Salomea. She sobbed:

"If only you could feel how my heart cries for you and for your unhappy love! We always saw right into each other's hearts; but now . . . now that you're suffering so, I'm unable to help you. I'm the one administering this blow! I'm driving a knife into the heart that brought back my son to me . . . Oh, Lord! Before I came here to say this, I shed endless tears. Oh yes . . . I almost forgot . . ."

The duchess looked for something in her pockets, saying:

"Don't be angry with me, and don't assume anything vulgar . . . I want to share with you everything I possess, spiritual and material. When I return home, you'll see for yourself what I mean. For the moment, this is half of what I have with me. You must take it! You must!"

The duchess put into Salomea's hand a fat, elongated purse filled with gold coins. She wrapped the young woman's fingers round the purse, raised her lifeless hand, and put the proffered treasure in the pocket of her dress.

Miss Salomea thought briefly: Ah—money . . . Her heart was transfixed by the news that he was going away forever and that she was staying here all alone. Beyond that was darkness. Like the echo of a thunderbolt, the older woman's words passed through her heart:

"Time will heal the wound . . ."

She immersed herself in the sound and meaning of those words—from her place of isolation far off. She longed to go away. To be alone! To run away somewhere! She murmured something inaudibly, her lips still resting on her mistress's shoulder. The duchess drew the young girl to her and put her arms about her. Profuse, unrestrained, truly maternal tears once again flowed from those powerful eyes onto Salomea's face. They were so genuine and so sincere that they brought a trace of solace to her wounded heart. They embraced each other and fell silent, gazing into the abyss of each other's feelings and plumbing the depths of each other's hearts.

Salomea still had the impression that she had already left that place and was going on a long journey somewhere. Her feelings crawled to some great height. She looked upon the other side that is never seen. She sighed as an unexpected thought came to her: So that's what the word "mother" means . . . She saw a mother's heart and all the emotions within it . . . She understood what a mother feels and the flow of her thoughts. She looked upon all this as upon the motionless earth and the clouds drifting overhead. She was amazed how many feelings there were within the mother, and what they were. She detected their twists and turns . . . A smile passed through all these distant sights, like the holy rays of the sun on a desolate region. She wanted to open her mouth and say that she too now had a child in her womb; but the outer word retreated in shame and disappeared in the depths of her heart.

The duchess closed her eyes and held Mija in her arms. She saw her feelings of love. They were almost her own feelings exactly. A flower-strewn meadow that human eyes see but once in a lifetime . . . Butterflies rise in the fragrant air, and multicolored grasses sway. A song of joy springs from a girl's lips as bare feet run in the meadow's dew.

And she was the one who was to cast the curse of death upon that piece of paradise, that divine element in human life; she was the one to trample the flowers, kill the butterflies, put out the light, and turn the scent of flowers into the stench of death!

She clenched her fists, hung her head over her young friend's shoulder, and wept as she saw it all. What was the purpose of the flowers and the sunlight? Why did she have to do that terrible thing? Why did she have to find within herself that monstrous courage and inexorable tyranny? Why did she have to raise her arm; why was it necessary for her to tighten her hand and choke the throat that she now held in a loving embrace?

A moan of profound anguish escaped her lips, and her words were stopped by her sobs.

XVII

It was in a different manner that Józef Odrowąż was persuaded of the necessity of leaving.

The duchess had not opposed the young man when he had spoken of rejoining the rebels—and the more his health and strength returned, the more impatient he became. She asked only that he be completely cured and in good health before he went off to fight again. And in order to recover fully, to get sufficient sleep after so many illnesses, and to put weight back on after he had grown so thin, he needed a couple of weeks of undisturbed nights and peaceful days. Where could that be had if not abroad?

His mother convinced him that, precisely so he would be able to return to the uprising as quickly as possible, he should travel with her first over the border to Kraków, and—provided with new clothes, arms, and military equipment, with a new commander and a new unit that she had apparently heard was being formed, and above all with newfound strength in body and soul—he would set forth.

The young man consented. He had no idea where his former unit was now. Where was he supposed to look for it? Who could tell him what was going on? Where could he obtain a half-decent gun? In Kraków he would look into the situation, find out how the uprising was progressing, look at a map, select a new unit, see new faces, and breathe with new hope. He wondered who was organizing the new unit that his mother had spoken of. How he longed to meet his commanding officer, an implacable, iron-handed strategist who would stamp his foot on the bloody earth and awaken the legions! The young duke's desire to fight was as profound and powerful as the sufferings he had lived through. His cold eyes stared into space and in it saw a Scythian war, a struggle to the death that the world knew nothing of and that had arisen from the degradation of

Poland. All memories faded within him, and only one craving remained: to stand in the ranks and follow orders.

As a result of these feelings, and because of the fear of searches, his mother's agitated state, and her fear of falling into the hands of the authorities at this stage, he agreed to depart without delay. Salomea did not hold him back. On the contrary, she encouraged him to go. A quiet smile hovered about her compressed lips as she urged him to leave . . . to rejoin the uprising. They spoke together of a wise, astute, firm, and fearless leader who must exist somewhere on earth, a Napoleon with the soul of a Machnicki. They spoke of a great battle that would put an end to bondage, redeem all that was painful, and make reparation for the wounds of those who had fallen and for their heroic deaths. What does a bullet in the head mean, if it is to happen—and in order for it to happen? Would it not be the greatest good fortune to perish at the place of rebirth from this ignominy?

He spoke of a statue in Paris that showed a dying soldier who in his last embrace puts his arm about the barrel of a cannon and passes away in this position. He told her of the ineffable fire that always penetrated his soul at the sight of that bronze soldier. That was joy. And now the same pure joy was within him as he was to return to arms.

Miss Salomea's eyes turned from fiery black to dull gray as she looked at him in her stupor. Now the duchess no longer left the two of them alone together. She became watchful and unshakable in her resolve. In that circle of three a bizarre music was to be played out on the taut strings of emotion. The young duke was in his ignorance moving toward his supposed action and for that action was sacrificing his love, trampling it without mercy into the ground. His mercilessness was as great as the merciless fate of Poland. He stared at Salomea with gritted teeth and a glittering smile on his lips.

Pupinetti sang at sunrise. The duke waved his hand at Mija, pointing to the bird. Everything was contained in that wave. And she understood perfectly. She answered his wave with a nod of her head. But at that very moment it occurred to her that she would have to open the cage and set the bird free—for how would she be able to bear his singing when she was left alone there? Let him fly to sunny lands, where her loved one would be! She bustled about, carefully putting Duchess Odrowąż's possessions in a strong leather bag. She busied herself with the torn handle of this valise, with trifling details, linen, the supplies for the journey that Szczepan had prepared.

Everything had happened so suddenly. At any moment there might be heard the hoofbeats of the soldiers coming to search the place, or the rumble of a carriage as it pulled up to whisk him away . . . to whisk him away forever. Ostensibly it was only to be for a certain time. Yet she was well aware that it would be forever. He himself would forget her in those distant lands. The noble duke . . . Now only God could turn everything about, break that fearsome will, foil those plans. He alone could send unexpected help, His all-powerful intervention—someone's death . . .

The departure was to take place at night, so as to cover as much as possible of the journey—the first stage, to the estate of the duchess's friends on the border—through the woods while it was still dark. The night magnified the terrible unease of the heart, which fell silent at some trite word of consolation, some phantasm of temporary brightness posing as calm. A great weight hanging by a thread . . . The hope of an unthinking person—What do I care?—expanded to the point of cynicism. She could feel her heart easing.

Then, imperceptibly, everything tumbled into a terrifying, mortal darkness. Her hair stood on end. Her madness gave off smoke clouds that burst into her feelings, while her frantic reason burned with tongues of fire. What was happening! In a moment there would be emptiness in this place! This direful house . . . Dominik would pass through the deserted rooms, stand at the empty bed of her lust, incline his head forward and back, listen intently to the song of the yellow bird, and laugh in an inaudible voice. How could she breathe here? How could she live? What was to be done?

She raised her eyes to the young man who had taken her life away and had himself become her life. With her eyes she professed to him the whole, boundless truth. Her lips would not say it—no, they would not! But the eyes have no power over the soul. He wept—he, who was noble and strong; he, who was not afraid of death and had begged for it many times; he, who now came to her boldly, certain that he was coming to her . . . Her heart was in a tumult of adoration. Those manly tears won her anew. The heart of your lover will not be untrue to itself and will not be untrue to you, Polish knight! It will be silent, whatever happens, to the very last moment! Standing at a distance, she raised his hair, his mouth, and his hands to her eyes and her mouth; with her eyes she gave him her body, her nakedness and her pride, her honor and her life, to the very last moment!

Józef Odrowąż was already dressed in his traveling clothes, looking quite the elegant gentleman; he was still unable to walk after his illness and shifted weakly from bed to couch and from couch to armchair. How changed he was! The clothes, which had been brought specially from the city, transformed him utterly. Was this the same man whose bloody wounds she had washed? He appeared before her now like a mournful bird never before seen or heard. The dark scar across his cheek beneath the eye gave him a lofty, half-divine appearance. His close-cropped hair made this new recruit look even younger. His eyes were ablaze, his mouth set. He was smiling . . .

He sat in the armchair and sank into it. His hands lay on the armrests, his head tipped back. Without raising that heavy head, staring from a distance at his mother and Miss Salomea, he hummed quietly, with his unshaken zeal:

> Down with titles, duke and master,
> Let's wipe away the years of shame . . .

Duchess Odrowąż stared back at him with a mild, benevolent smile, for a moment. Then she began fiddling with her things and his with a redoubled energy, no longer even for a moment leaving the room where he and Salomea sat. These two by now were enveloped in a mantle of calm and had retreated within themselves.

But at one point Miss Brynicka remembered something. An inner spring rose up and forced its way through her outward torpor as if through a shell. She stirred uneasily. She wanted to do something, to act in some way, to say something . . . She felt stifled. She began to stretch herself in a painful yawn. Oh, that was it! That's right! That's right! She sought the bullet sewn into the bodice of her dress. She tore open the seam with her fingernails and pried out the lead ball that had come out of Józef's wound. She planted a short, unostentatious kiss on the lump of Muscovite lead. She put it into Duchess Odrowąż's hand. Stammering, unable to find the right words, through chattering teeth she managed to say politely and calmly:

"This bullet . . . it's from me . . . as a keepsake! . . ."

The duchess took the bullet and weighed it in her beautiful, delicate white hand. Her wise brow was furrowed as she fell deep in thought. She looked into Salomea's face with eyes dismal from suffering. How painful to her was the girl's vengeful gesture!

The young duke was extremely worried by the gift of the bullet.

Something touched him; something flashed before his eyes. He braced his emaciated arms on the armrests of the chair in order to stand. He looked into his mother's face with the eyes of an inquisitor. His mother shook her head limply. It was as if she had been shot through with that bullet. Her hands trembled. Józef wanted to leap up and ask questions, when suddenly a rumble was heard . . . Everyone ran out onto the veranda. A traveling carriage without lanterns stood before them. To Salomea's eyes, its shape, and the outline of the four horses, appeared like a vision of the chariot of death.

With an inward groan she leaned against the wall. A man in coachman's livery gave the agreed word. Hurriedly, as quickly as possible, they let the horses graze for a short time, brought out the luggage, and fastened it onto the carriage. The duchess and her son briefly said good-bye to everyone and stepped into the carriage. It moved away from the veranda slowly and quietly, step by step, so as not to make a noise with the rumble of wheels or the sound of hoofbeats. It was engulfed in the darkness of the night. It disappeared.

Mrs. Rudecka, tired and, as usual, melancholy, left the veranda at once, relieved that the dangerous guest had at last been taken away. Szczepan, who had helped to load the valise, also went off. Miss Salomea was left alone. She stared at the point in the darkness that had swallowed up the carriage. Her knees were pressed together, her hands folded on her lap. Her heart was calm.

An unexpected turn in the world of her feelings led her to think with a certain satisfaction about the money Duchess Odrowąż had given her. These thoughts acted as a compress on her heart, stifling any emotions. The moment the very thought of which had crushed her soul, the moment of departure, had gone, passed, with virtually no feeling whatsoever. Salomea's mind passed timidly over it all—the empty room, the canary's cage, her fear of Dominik—and in amazement she observed that everything had become painless and all her feelings had been dulled.

The idea that there was so much money brought her a hideous relief . . . If her father had been alive, he would probably have been delighted! For it had been earned honestly, by a genuine service. He would no longer have been the poor steward, always in the same jacket and the same high-topped boots, never sleeping enough or eating enough, trailing on horseback from farm to farm every day of the week, always facing quarrels and quandaries, always outdoors come rain or shine, worrying about someone else's profits . . . Who knew if for this much money it wouldn't have been possible to lease a property elsewhere, a small place where a person could set up his own farm? . . . There would be livestock, draft horses, and a pair of fine horses for traveling, a sprung trap for church, and Sunday clothes. The country folk would call him "the squire" when they saw him . . .

Her thoughts wandered about that unknown place. But she had to return from the land of aimless daydreams to coarse reality; so she gradually began to think about his distant grave. Oh, to go there on her knees, to seek out the grave, to fall upon it and put her arms about it! To tell that mound of earth what had happened, to confess to it her awful, base, shameful sin! To explain her fall and disclose her guilt! She should use these gold coins to purchase an iron cross for the grave and to put up an inscription . . .

She began to wonder how she would find the place. She recalled the last letter, written with the lead bullet, and remembered that it mentioned the name of the villager who had taken her father in before he died. She took the letter from her pocket and held it in her hand. The night was so dark that she couldn't read her father's final words. Her hands fell to her sides.

But at this moment the hand of God began to draw aside the

thick curtain of night from the earth. The silhouettes of the alder trees began to emerge from the darkness, with their crowns bent in various directions on their lofty trunks—strange, unexpected shapes like the forms of painful feelings. These figures etched against the sky drew one's gaze to themselves, but only for a moment—for that gaze suddenly broke away . . . In the distance, the gray light of dawn separated the earth from the sky. Soft mists glimmered in a tawny blur over the channel of the river. Birds began to sing in the haze, so harmoniously that it seemed as if the image of the mist itself in the gloaming was announcing its presence and expressing its color and its form. A gentle wind, moist from the lowlands, shook the sleepy branches. Close by, whitish colors appeared in the flower beds of the garden. These hues stung her heart with a memory, and she beheld herself like a naked pain made visible. But her dauntless eyes overcame it. She had to absorb vengeance and become only herself. It passed . . .

An oppressive drowsiness overcame her body and her soul. Now, at last, after all her misadventures she would be able to catch up on her sleep in her own bed, which for so long had been taken by a stranger. Her heart would no longer tremble at the knocking on the window. Let them come and look, let them go poking around and searching! There would be no more insane hardships, no more perpetual running to and fro and endless, sleepless anguish. There was no one to watch over anymore. There would be peace, quiet, order. To sleep . . .

Salomea stood up to carry out her intention and go to her room. Yet instead, after a short hesitation, she went to take a walk by the river. She was driven by the expectation that before she reached the water's edge, it would be light enough to read in her father's letter the name of the village and that of the farmer in whose cottage he had died. She went slowly down the road, on the soft sand that the nighttime dew had made damp, covering it with a dark coating.

Then she set out across the wet grass, and without knowing why, she walked down toward the river.

For a moment she stopped and stood in the arbor overgrown with wild vines. Her thoughts were calm and restrained, revolving around what she would buy with the money and what she would be able to treat herself to. She dwelled with pride on the idea that she would no longer be a drudge dependent on the goodwill of distant relatives—an orphan whom any man who visited could try to kiss. Now they would have to bestir themselves; they'd have to beat the competition before she would deign to speak to any of them . . .

Dawn was breaking slowly and imperceptibly. The birdsong sounded louder. Unmown flower-strewn meadows could be seen in the distance, slaked with dull-sheened dew. Droplets hung on petals and stems, gray as balls of quicksilver. The far-off woods were blue. The red glow intensified in the multicolored sky. Salomea left the arbor and walked to the river, which had swelled to fill its banks from the St. John's Day rains. The turbid water was the color of clay and coursed in whirling eddies. The red and yellow flowers were covered in silt, while the overhanging stalks were bent double, and the current had swept up the alder thickets, the willows, and the osiers. A wet smell rose from the place, with the intensified scent of countless herbs.

In the profound quiet of the morning Salomea suddenly heard a distant sound: a brief thudding like the far-off beat of a drum. She listened intently and nodded. It was the carriage that bore the duchess and her son, crossing the bridge over the very same river far away across the meadows, near the woods. It was the hoofbeats of four harnessed horses and the rumble of the carriage wheels over the logs of the bridge. She sank into thought at this sound.

And all at once her soul was rent within her like the warp of a piece of cloth torn apart by the hands of a demon. An indescribable despair, blind and deaf, wild as a tiger's hunger as it pounces on its prey, issued from that unknown hiding place in her soul. Her body, frantic and unthinking, ran along the twisting riverbank, to the left and to the right. After a while, in a certain place Salomea drew up short. She stared at the stormy, turbulent water with its swirling reddish bubbles. She thought and thought . . .

Some iron thing within her rose up, unseated her very being, and caused it to move. She laughed aloud. From her pocket she took the duchess's purse, filled with gold coins; she poured some of them into her hand and, raising her arm, hurled them into the racing water. The water responded with a splash.

Salomea poured the remainder of the coins out of the purse and again cast them like seeds into the racing water.

The water responded with a splash. It alone understood the torments of her heart. It alone echoed them with a sound that she in turn understood. Once she had attended to the money, Salomea left the place. She wandered through tall grass wet from the dew. She stared at the luxuriant flowers, which seemed to feel sorry for her yet were unable to help her. She tried to get out to a dry place, because her shoes were soaked through. She found herself on the sandy road that led from the manor to the nearest bridge. Daylight was breaking, and it revealed the deep tracks of carriage wheels and horses' hooves in the wet sand. When she saw these fresh tracks, white on the dew-darkened sand, she stopped and sank into thought again. Something within her was bursting, tearing her apart . . .

She walked slowly toward the house. But her foot stumbled against some small rock. And in this way she fell face down in the wet sand.

Old Szczepan rose at dawn as he did every day and took the buckets to fetch water from the spring that from time immemorial had risen under the pear tree on the hillside. As he did every day, he muttered to himself as he rattled the buckets. He turned off the road onto the path that was a shortcut to the spring. Then suddenly, glancing at the road, he noticed something black lying there. He was struck by a premonition that it was some poor fellow from the Polish army. He was already moving away—someone else would find him . . . But purely out of curiosity he walked up cautiously. And once he got close enough to see clearly, he flung the buckets to the ground and rushed up to her as fast as his legs would carry him. He carefully raised the limp body from the ground in his strong arms, leaned the drooping head over his shoulder, and carried her gently back to the house, muttering:

"What is it, you poor little thing? What is it? The old man knew, oh yes, he did . . . They did you a bad turn, I can see—they hurt you good and proper—they did you wrong good and proper! . . ."

European Classics

M. Ageyev
Novel with Cocaine

Jerzy Andrzejewski
Ashes and Diamonds

Honoré de Balzac
The Bureaucrats

Andrei Bely
Kotik Letaev

Heinrich Böll
Absent without Leave
And Never Said a Word
And Where Were You, Adam?
The Bread of Those Early Years
End of a Mission
Irish Journal
Missing Persons and Other Essays
The Safety Net
A Soldier's Legacy
The Stories of Heinrich Böll
Tomorrow and Yesterday
The Train Was on Time
What's to Become of the Boy?
Women in a River Landscape

Madeleine Bourdouxhe
La Femme de Gilles

Karel Čapek
Nine Fairy Tales
War with the Newts

Lydia Chukovskaya
Sofia Petrovna

Grazia Deledda
After the Divorce
Elias Portolu

Leonid Dobychin
The Town of N

Yury Dombrovsky
The Keeper of Antiquities

Aleksandr Druzhinin
Polinka Saks • The Story of Aleksei Dmitrich

Venedikt Erofeev
Moscow to the End of the Line

Konstantin Fedin
Cities and Years

Arne Garborg
Weary Men

Fyodor Vasilievich Gladkov
Cement

I. Grekova
The Ship of Widows

Vasily Grossman
Forever Flowing

Stefan Heym
The King David Report
The Wandering Jew

Marek Hlasko
The Eighth Day of the Week

Bohumil Hrabal
Closely Watched Trains

Ilf and Petrov
The Twelve Chairs

Vsevolod Ivanov
Fertility and Other Stories

Erich Kästner
Fabian: The Story of a Moralist

Valentine Kataev
Time, Forward!

Kharms and Vvedensky
The Man with the Black Coat: Russia's Literature of the Absurd

Danilo Kiš
The Encyclopedia of the Dead
Hourglass

Ignacy Krasicki
The Adventures of Mr. Nicholas Wisdom

Miroslav Krleza
The Return of Philip Latinowicz

Curzio Malaparte
Kaputt
The Skin

Karin Michaëlis
The Dangerous Age

Neera
Teresa

V. F. Odoevsky
Russian Nights

Andrey Platonov
The Foundation Pit

Bolesław Prus
The Sins of Childhood and Other Stories

Valentin Rasputin
Farewell to Matyora

Alain Robbe-Grillet
Snapshots

Arthur Schnitzler
The Road to the Open

Yury Trifonov
Disappearance

Evgeniya Tur
Antonina

Ludvík Vaculík
The Axe

Vladimir Voinovich
The Life and Extraordinary Adventures of Private Ivan Chonkin
Pretender to the Throne

Stefan Żeromski
The Faithful River

Lydia Zinovieva-Annibal
The Tragic Menagerie

Stefan Zweig
Beware of Pity